P9-DNM-683

MYSTERY OF THE MOSS-COVERED MANSION

A friend of Carson Drew's has been arrested and charged with sending a truck loaded with explosive oranges into the Space Center complex at Cape Kennedy. Knowing that Mr. Billington could not possibly be guilty of sabotage, Nancy and her father rush to the defense of the accused man.

During the Drews' investigation Nancy becomes suspicious of an old, spooky mansion. Behind a high, steel-mesh enclosure fierce African wild animals roam over the extensive grounds. Through a ruse the clever teen-age detective discovers that something besides the training of wild animals is going on at the mysterious moss-covered mansion estate.

Many dangerous moments await Nancy before she proves Mr. Billington's innocence and thwarts the plans of treacherous subversives bent on undermining the U. S. space program.

Orange trees were burning everywhere

NANCY DREW MYSTERY STORIES®

Mystery of the Moss-Covered Mansion

BY CAROLYN KEENE

GROSSET & DUNLAP
Publishers • New York
A member of The Putnam & Grosset Group

Acknowledgement is made to Mildred Wirt Benson, who under the pen name
Carolyn Keene, wrote the original NANCY DREW books

Copyright © 1971, 1969, 1941 by Simon & Schuster, Inc. All rights reserved.
Published by Grosset & Dunlap, Inc., a member of The Putnam & Grosset Group,
New York. Published simultaneously in Canada. Printed in the U.S.A.
NANCY DREW MYSTERY STORIES® is a registered trademark of Simon & Schuster,
Inc. GROSSET & DUNLAP is a trademark of Grosset & Dunlap, Inc.
Library of Congress Catalog Card Number: 77-155244 ISBN 978-0-448-09518-9
9 10 8

Contents

Mystery
of the
Moss-Covered Mansion

CHAPTER I

The Crash

THE Drews' living room was in semidarkness as Nancy walked in. Only one lamp was lighted. Under its glow her father sat absorbed in a single sheet of newspaper which lay across his knees.

On the table next to him were a pad and pencil. Figures, letters, and symbols were scrawled on the top sheet.

Nancy stopped beside his chair. "Crossword puzzle?" asked the reddish-blond haired girl.

Mr. Drew, a tall, good-looking man, glanced up at his attractive, eighteen-year-old daughter and smiled. "No, it's not a crossword puzzle. Actually it's a message in a personal column from this Florida newspaper."

"A personal?" Nancy repeated. "But why are you making all these hieroglyphics on the pad?"

"Sit down and I'll show you," her father said.

Nancy pulled up the chair from the opposite

1

side of the table. Her father was the leading attorney in River Heights where they lived and she was sure he was puzzling over some problem in connection with his work.

She asked, "Dad, are you busy on a regular case or one with a mystery?"

Mr. Drew laughed. "A case with a mystery. I sent to Florida for newspapers of several weeks back, thinking I might pick up a clue from them."

He handed the paper to Nancy and pointed out an item in the personal column. "What does my detective daughter think?" he asked.

Nancy studied the unusual message. Finally she read the ad aloud:

" *'Son of fruit grower wishes forgiveness. Will return money.'* "

The young sleuth was silent for several seconds, then she frowned. "This could or could not be suspicious. Maybe some father and son had a difference of opinion and he ran away, taking some of his dad's money. He put this ad in the paper, expecting his father to see it and forgive him."

Mr. Drew did not reply. He picked up a sheet from another newspaper dated several days later. He pointed to it and said, "Do you think this one makes as much sense as the other?"

The second ad was longer. It said, *"Natural color oranges best antidote for grower's son's special kind of chronic asthma."*

"This one sounds more like a code than the first," Nancy remarked.

Her father asked, "Do you see any connection between the two messages?"

"Yes, one. Both items contain the words son and grower." Nancy looked up at her father. "Dad, do you know what it means and are you teasing me to see if I can figure it out?"

Mr. Drew chuckled. "Such a thing would have been a temptation," he said, "but this time I confess I haven't the faintest idea what these personals mean. The fact that the words son and grower appear in both makes me suspect that they're code messages."

"And you have a hunch they may relate to your case?" Nancy inquired. Her father nodded.

Nancy picked up a sheet of paper and began to jot down letters and numbers. Mr. Drew watched her, always intrigued by the way his daughter tackled a code. Nancy had made a study of codes and he was sure she would soon find the answer to this puzzle.

There was silence for a minute, then suddenly Nancy exclaimed, "Here's a hidden message that makes sense!"

As she leaned across the table to show it to her father, they heard a terrific crash directly in front of the house.

"Oh!" said Nancy. "A car accident!"

She was already dashing across the room to the

front door. Mr. Drew followed her through the spacious hall and outside into the autumn night. They could vaguely see two cars locked together. The Drews raced down their curving driveway to the street.

Nancy and her father were appalled by what they saw. One car had smashed through the hood of the other. The lone occupant, a man, was slumped over the steering wheel, unconscious.

Looking into the other car, Nancy exclaimed, "Bess! George!"

Bess Marvin and George Fayne were cousins and Nancy's closest friends. Their parents had gone away together for a few days and Bess and George had come to the Drews to stay.

"Girls, how dreadful!" Nancy cried out. "We'll get you into the house right away and call a doctor."

George, who had been driving, was unbuckling her seat belt. The safety belts and shoulder straps the cousins were wearing had saved them from being thrown against the windshield.

Bess was quivering with fright, but George was angry. "That crazy driver!" she said indignantly. "He suddenly came whizzing across the street and smashed into us! I don't need a doctor! Just a new car!"

Mr. Drew said, "I'm sorry about this, girls, but fortunately you seem to be all right. Nevertheless,

"How dreadful!" Nancy exclaimed

I insist that you have your family doctor look you over. Nancy, suppose you take Bess and George inside and call Dr. Clifford."

By this time the Drews' housekeeper, kindly Hannah Gruen, had come from the house to see what the commotion was.

Recognizing Bess and George, she said worriedly, "My goodness! What happened?"

Mr. Drew answered. "George can explain later. Right now, will you notify the police to come at once? I'll go over and see if I can do anything for that man."

Hannah hurried into the house and called headquarters. Then she dialed Dr. Clifford's number. The girls had followed her. Bess, a blonde, was naturally pink-cheeked, but now she looked like a ghost. George nervously paced the floor, though she said her legs felt like rubber.

"Please sit down, George," urged Nancy, "and try to relax."

Just then a police car arrived. Nancy ran outside to join her father. He introduced officers Hampton and Russo.

"This young man," said Mr. Drew, "lost control of his car. He seems to be in bad shape."

Officer Hampton leaned over to examine the man. He straightened up and nodded. "You're right, Mr. Drew. I believe this guy is under the influence of some drug. Probably he passed out before he hit the other car."

A moment later Dr. Clifford drove up. The officers asked him to give his opinion about the victim. After a quick examination, the physician agreed with Hampton's diagnosis and declared the young man should go to the hospital at once.

"We'll take him there," said Russo.

Meanwhile Hampton had been making notes and snapping pictures of the two cars. He helped Russo lift the victim into the police car.

"Mr. Drew," he called, "will you phone a towing company to haul these cars away at once? They're blocking the street. If you have no luck, let me know."

"I'll be glad to," the lawyer replied.

Russo said they would return as soon as possible from the hospital, and get a statement from Bess and George.

When the others entered the house, the cousins greeted Dr. Clifford with hugs. He had brought them both into the world and they were very fond of him.

The doctor chuckled. "You girls don't seem very sick," he said, "but let me examine you." Mr. Drew left the room. In a few minutes the physician said, "No broken bones or sprains. Nevertheless, it's bed for you, Bess and George, as soon as the police talk with you. I'd say go now, but I suppose the law has to come first!"

Shortly after he had left, the two officers returned. Officer Hampton did the questioning while his partner took notes. The session was soon over and the men left.

Bess and George went to bed, but Nancy and her father stayed up to wait for the towing company truck. It was midnight when they turned out the lights and retired.

The evening's excitement had interrupted the discussion of Mr. Drew's case and the suspicious personals in the Florida newspaper. But immediately after church the next morning it was resumed.

"Nancy, what was it you were going to tell me last night about the coded message?" he asked.

"I think I've figured out the first one you showed me. The message in it is, 'Son wishes money.' "

"It could be," her father agreed. "What method were you using?"

His daughter smiled. "Words 1, 5, 9, and 13."

The other girls were intensely interested.

Bess had picked up the second personal and tried to make sense out of it. She wrinkled her forehead. "What in the world does 'Natural antidote special asthma' mean?"

"Nothing," Nancy replied, "but how about using only the first letters of those words?"

George exclaimed, "They spell NASA!"

The others looked at Nancy in astonishment, and Bess cried out, "NASA? The National Aeronautics Space Administration?"

"Yes," the young sleuth answered. "I believe it refers to the Kennedy Space Center in Florida!"

Mr. Drew looked grim. "Now I'm convinced the personals relate to my case," he said. "Explosives were shipped into the base hidden inside oranges in sacks. I must get down there at once! I was wondering if—"

As her father paused, a thought raced through Nancy's mind. Was he debating if he should take her along?

CHAPTER II

Suspicious Message

NANCY watched her father's face carefully as he stared out the window. She knew he was trying to make up his mind about something important. Finally he turned toward his daughter.

"I could use some help in solving the mystery of the explosive oranges."

"And," Nancy said hopefully, "you think I might be able to help?"

The lawyer nodded. "My client, Mr. Billington, was arrested for bringing explosive Hamlin oranges into the Space Center. He is out on bail but his case is coming up soon. He's innocent. Mr. Billington owns a grove on Merritt Island, which produces only Pineapple Oranges. Someone secretly borrowed a truck of his and delivered several sacks of Hamlin oranges to the Center. The person presented an official card bearing Mr. Billington's name, and signed a slip with his signature. Of course it was a forgery."

Mr. Drew went on, "Unfortunately I can't represent him in Florida because I have no license to practice in that state. My main reason for going down is to engage the services of a Florida lawyer. He and I will work together on the legal angle. I can't stay long this time because I have other urgent matters coming up. But the mysterious culprit must be found before the trial."

Nancy could not refrain from saying, "Dad, if you can't remain on Merritt Island, how about Bess and George and Hannah and I making the trip and staying there?"

"Just what I was thinking," her father replied. "Mr. Billington received special permission from the authorities to leave Florida and come North to sign for the purchase of some property. The buyer is going to Europe, so the transaction had to be made at once.

"Mr. Billington has offered me the use of his house and car and invited anyone else I would like to bring along. He and Mrs. Billington are on their way now but they have a caretaker and his wife who live in the residence. They're Antin and Tina Resardo. She takes care of the house and does the cooking. Antin is foreman of the grove and the sorting and packing house."

Bess and George said they would love to go but would have to obtain permission from their parents. George made the long-distance call. First she told her father about the accident and the wrecked car. "But Bess and I are okay."

"It's too bad about the car, but I'm glad you and Bess weren't hurt," he replied. "George, report the damage immediately to our insurance agent, Mr. Dowley."

"All right, Dad." George now told him about the proposed trip.

"That sounds great!" Mr. Fayne said. "I'll ask the Marvins." He came back to the phone, saying, "It's okay. Have a good time."

George spoke to her mother and Bess talked to her parents. When she finished, George phoned the insurance man and within fifteen minutes he was at the Drew house. She gave Mr. Dowley all the details and he promised to take charge of the matter.

"You go on to Florida and have fun," he said. "When do you leave?"

George went to find Mr. Drew and asked him. He smiled. "I'd like to hop a plane this afternoon," he said. "Do you think you could be ready?"

George looked at her watch. "It will take me about twenty minutes to pack some lightweight clothes and my swimsuit."

It was decided that the group would have an early lunch at the Drews' and leave immediately afterward. While they were eating, the telephone rang. Nancy answered it.

The others heard her exclaim, "Ned! How good to hear from you. Where are you?"

From there on Ned did most of the talking. He was an attractive Emerson College football player who dated Nancy exclusively.

When she came back to the table, her eyes were sparkling. "Great news!" she announced. "You know Ned's parents have had a house on Merritt Island for some time. Mr. and Mrs. Nickerson are there right now and they're going to have a house party. Bess and George, you're invited, as well as myself, and Ned will bring Burt and Dave along."

Burt Eddleton and Dave Evans were George's and Bess's favorite dates. They, too, went to Emerson College.

"Fabulous!" Bess exclaimed.

"Super!" George added.

Nancy remarked, "We'll have time to work on the mystery before the house party starts."

Mr. Drew chuckled. "Well, we'd better leave. I'll load your luggage in the car, while you girls tidy up the kitchen. Hannah, will you see that all the doors and windows are locked and the burglar alarm set?"

The housekeeper hurried off to do this. Then the travelers grabbed their coats and left the house. On the way to the local airport, Mr. Drew said they had a choice of flying either to Orlando or Melbourne, Florida. "Melbourne is a little closer to Merritt Island so I've chosen that one. We land at Kennedy Airport there. I phoned the Billington house and asked Tina if she and Antin would meet us. She agreed."

Hours later, when the Drews and their friends reached Melbourne, they looked everywhere for the couple. No one fitting their description was around. Finally only one elderly woman and a naval officer were left in the passenger waiting room.

"I think I'll telephone the house and see what happened," Mr. Drew said.

He closed himself into a phone booth and tried for ten minutes to get an answer. At last he came outside.

"No one was there, so maybe the Resardos are on the way. I guess we'll just have to wait."

An hour passed and still Antin and Tina had not arrived. Mr. Drew was annoyed. "We'll have to take a taxi," he said. "It'll be an expensive trip. I wonder what happened to the Resardos."

The group enjoyed the ride past the many beautiful homes and glimmering lakes and inlets, some small, others large. When they reached Cocoa the driver went across the bridge to Merritt Island, then along various winding roads. Finally the taxi pulled up in front of a large Spanish-type house on the Indian River. The ground floor had a patio across the front and on one side. There were several chairs under a small grove of shade trees.

While Mr. Drew was paying the taximan, Nancy went to the front door and rapped with the knocker. The visitors stood waiting but no one came to let them in.

George walked to the rear of the dwelling and pressed a buzzer at the back door. No response. She rejoined the others.

"Nobody home," she announced, and dropped into a garden chair. Her companions also seated themselves and waited. About twenty minutes later a car pulled into the driveway and a couple got out.

As they approached the visitors, the man said, "We are the Resardos. Where have you been?"

Mr. Drew looked directly at Tina. "Exactly where I asked you to meet us."

The woman rolled her eyes toward her husband but did not speak. He said angrily, "You told my wife we were to meet you at Orlando but you weren't there."

"I told her Melbourne," Mr. Drew replied, "but never mind. Just let us into the house, please. How much time do we have to unpack before dinner?"

Antin glared at the newcomers. "My wife has a bad headache and must lie down. You people will have to get your own dinner."

He unlocked the front door, ushered Tina in, and followed her.

"Warm reception," Bess whispered to the other girls.

"I can foresee trouble with that couple," George replied.

Tina went upstairs, but Antin stalked to the back door and went out. He walked off to the right into a large orange grove.

The newcomers climbed the stairs and chose bedrooms. They found that one was closed and locked and assumed this must lead to the Resardos' quarters.

After unpacking, Hannah and the girls located the kitchen and examined the contents of the refrigerator. There was plenty of food for a good meal and Hannah chose a big pot of chicken cooked with rice and gravy. The girls set the table in the flower-papered dining room, which had a large glass-top table and white wicker chairs.

When the meal was ready, Antin walked in. Without saying a word, he took one of the plates warming on the stove and helped himself to a very generous portion of everything. He then filled a second plate with food.

He said to Hannah, "I'm taking this up to my wife. We'll eat in our room."

The others assembled in the dining room and after grace had been said by Mr. Drew, they began to eat the delicious dinner. Before they had reached the dessert course, Antin came down the stairs carrying the empty plates, which he put into the sink.

The others heard him open a cabinet door and knew he was getting plates for the dessert, which was an apple pie. The visitors were aghast to see Antin going through the hall with at least half the pie on two plates!

After he had gone upstairs, George burst out, "What's eating him?"

Bess giggled. "Nothing. He's eating everything."

Nancy jumped up and went out to look at the pie. The portion that was left, if cut into five slices, would give each person a piece one-inch wide!

"That man is the limit," she complained to Hannah, who had followed her.

"He certainly is," the housekeeper agreed, "and I suppose he expects me to wash his dirty dishes."

A little later Antin returned and left two empty plates. Nancy stopped him. Eager to start work on the mystery at once, she asked him what he knew about Mr. Billington's case.

The caretaker scowled. "Nothing that you don't know," he replied and went outdoors.

From the window Nancy saw him go into the orange grove. Dusk had fallen and she could not see which direction he had taken.

After the dishes had been put into the washer

and the dining room vacuumed for crumbs, George said that she and Bess had promised to let their parents know of the girls' safe arrival.

"I'll do it," Bess offered and went to the rear of the hall. As she picked up the phone, the unfamiliar voice of a man was saying, "You know what to do next. Keep your eye on all visitors."

Bess hung up and came back to the living room to report the conversation. "Are the Billingtons on a party line?" she asked.

"No," Mr. Drew answered. He frowned. "I don't like this. There must be an extension phone and somebody in this place is talking on it."

"I'll check!" Nancy offered.

She knew there was no other phone on the first floor, so she started to climb to the second. Halfway up the stairs, she heard a door close softly. She ran the rest of the way and walked along the hall. There was an extension in Mr. Billington's bedroom but nobody was there. The Resardos' door was closed.

"Perhaps Tina was using the phone up here," Nancy thought.

What had the message meant? she wondered. And were she and her father and her friends the "visitors" that the man had referred to? Nancy went downstairs and told the others her suspicions.

"There's probably another extension outside somewhere," Nancy said. "Perhaps in the orange packing house! Let's see if anyone's there!"

CHAPTER III

Spooky Grounds

WHEN Nancy rushed from the rear entrance of the Billington home, she headed for the orange grove. A distance beyond she could see a wavering light and assumed that someone with a flashlight was walking among the trees.

"I wonder who the person is?" she asked herself. "Antin?"

When George and Mr. Drew caught up to Nancy, they said Bess had remained with Hannah. Nancy mentioned the light. They had not noticed it and now the beam had vanished.

The three had left in such a hurry they had neglected to bring flashlights. As they progressed deeper into the grove, the searchers could see practically nothing under the trees.

"We'll never be able to find the orange packing house," George remarked.

They went on for several seconds, then Nancy stopped. "I guess you're right. We'll come back in the morning and find out if there is an extension in the packing house. I'm inclined to believe it was Antin calling from there. What do you two think?"

Mr. Drew agreed, but George said, "It might have been Tina. Don't forget, Nancy, that you heard a door close softly."

Nancy made no reply. She had turned to go back to the house but suddenly realized she did not know which direction to take. She consulted her companions.

Mr. Drew laughed. "I should think a detective like you could find her way in the dark," he teased.

"Just for that," said his daughter, "I'll lead you right back to the Billingtons'."

She began to feel the tree trunks, saying to herself, "We came north and that would be the roughest side of the tree." Presently she found the south side and then said, "Follow me!"

The trees, though planted in straight rows, were not in lines parallel to the compass. Nancy felt the bark of each tree she came to and kept veering slightly eastward. In a little while the lights of the Billington house came into view.

"You did it!" George praised her friend.

Nancy laughed. "I played leader this time but either of you could have found the way."

When the three came into the kitchen they were greeted by Hannah and Bess. "Mission accomplished?" Mrs. Gruen asked.

"I'm afraid not," Nancy replied. Then she whispered, "Has Antin come in?"

Bess replied, "Yes. He rushed past the two of us without saying a word and went upstairs. He sure is a weirdo."

In low voices the group discussed the Resardos. While they had no proof the couple was dishonest, each of them had a feeling of mistrust. Hannah suggested that as a safety precaution the visitors lock their bedroom doors. Everyone looked at Mr. Drew. Would he agree to lock his?

To their surprise he did. He said no more, but the others were sure Nancy's father was taking no chances with the caretaker and his wife in the house. The night passed peacefully, however.

When the Drews and their friends assembled for breakfast, Antin and Tina had not yet come downstairs. Just as the group finished eating, the couple appeared. They said good morning but carried on no conversation. They helped themselves to the food Hannah had left on the stove and ate in the kitchen.

Presently Antin went out the rear door. Tina announced she was going shopping and did not offer to help with the housework. She hurried away.

Hannah Gruen was exasperated. "How long

does that woman expect me to wash her dirty dishes and prepare meals?"

"I'll speak to them later," Mr. Drew promised. "I'm leaving now in Mr. Billington's car to see Mr. Datsun, the lawyer I engaged to help me on the case."

Tina had already left in the Resardos' car. Was she going grocery shopping or on some errands of her own?

"I don't know whether to buy any supplies or not," said Hannah. "What do you think, girls?"

Bess, who was hungry most of the time, answered, "I vote we buy some food and not depend on that awful creature."

"But how are we going to get it?" George spoke up. "We have no car."

Mrs. Gruen sighed. "I guess we can make out until your father returns and you can borrow the car."

As soon as the necessary housework was finished, the girls set off through the orange grove to find the packing house. It was a good distance ahead. On the way Nancy and her friends saw many men picking oranges and putting them into baskets. A small truck would pick them up.

The packing house at the far end of the grove was a long, rectangular building. It contained machinery for sorting oranges by size, cartons for mailing fruit, and net sacks for local delivery.

Men and women were busy picking out defective fruit.

There was a glass-partitioned office in one corner. On the desk stood a telephone!

Nancy walked up to one of the men and inquired if Antin was around. She learned he had not been there all morning.

"I can't say when he'll be back," the workman continued. "He stays away from here a good deal nowadays. But that's all right. We get along without him."

The girls looked questioningly at one another but made no comment. Nancy asked the man, "Is the telephone here on a separate line or is it an extension of the one at the house?"

"It's an intercom system with four extensions on this one number. Two of them are in the house. A third is at the side of this building. Would you like to make a call?" he asked.

"Yes, I would," Nancy replied, glad of the chance to let her eyes roam around the office desk for a clue to the mysterious phone conversation.

She was disappointed not to find any, but Hannah Gruen had a message for her.

"Mrs. Nickerson called. She said something of interest has come up and she wants you to stop over as soon as possible."

"She didn't say what it was?" Nancy queried.

"No," Hannah replied.

Nancy said the girls would visit Mrs. Nickerson when they could use Mr. Billington's car. "We'll see you in a little while, Hannah."

She and her friends watched the sorting and packing operation. Nancy spoke to several of the workers. Not one of them could give any information about the identity of the man who had delivered the oranges with the explosives in them. All the men declared they knew nothing about it except what had been in the newspapers. One thing they were sure of—Mr. Billington was innocent. They hoped he would soon be exonerated.

The girls heard a truck arriving and went outside to watch it being unloaded. Baskets of oranges were lifted onto a belt which carried them to a chute where the fruit was dumped into the washing and sorting machine.

Nancy stood near the truck, gazing at the man who was lifting out the baskets. Suddenly one slipped from his hands and came tumbling directly toward Nancy's head!

"Look out!" cried Bess behind her.

Fortunately Nancy had seen the basket and leaped out of the way. The fruit smashed to the ground. Her first thought was that the man had dropped it on purpose, then she rationalized what possible purpose could he have in harming her? He did not apologize. Nancy went inside and asked a workman his name.

"It's Jackson," he replied. "We call him Old

Clumsy Fingers." Nancy smiled and said that explained why she had almost been hit with a basket
of oranges.

Nancy, Bess, and George walked back through
the grove, disappointed that they had learned
nothing to advance their sleuthing.

As they approached the house, Nancy told the
girls about Mrs. Nickerson's call. "But we can't
go there without a car. It's too far. I hope Dad will
be back soon."

When he had not returned by late morning,
Nancy became restless. She was on the verge of
telephoning Mrs. Nickerson, when George, who
had been exploring the grounds, dashed into the
house.

"Guess what I saw!" she explained. "The Billingtons' boat. It's neat! Why don't we go to the
Nickersons in that?"

"Great idea!" Bess spoke up. "Let's see if it will
run."

Nancy told Hannah where the girls were going,
then the three hurried through the Billingtons'
lovely garden to the waterfront. Only a few motor-
boats were purring along the shores of the Indian
River.

The end of the garden was several feet above
the water level and had a bulkhead to keep the
soil from washing away. A boathouse extended
into the river. Inside it was a sleek speedboat, the
Starbeam. The key was in the ignition.

"What a beauty!" Bess cried out. "But it looks powerful. Nancy, would you dare take it out?"

The young detective smiled. "Of course."

She made sure there was sufficient fuel and familiarized herself with the various gadgets. Her eyes twinkling, she said, "Here goes!"

In a few seconds the motor was throbbing quietly and she steered the craft into the river. Twenty minutes later she pulled alongside a dock which bore the name Nickerson. The girls tied the boat securely and went up to the house.

Ned's mother was a very attractive woman. When greeting Nancy she showed the deep affection she held for the girl.

"What I wanted to tell you," Mrs. Nickerson said as they all sipped glasses of cola, "is that friends of ours who have gone North to live have put their house on the market. It's listed with Mr. Gilbert Scarlett, a local realtor. I was thinking how wonderful it would be, Nancy, if your father would buy the place."

"I'd love to see it," Nancy replied. "Is it far from here?"

"No, we can walk there easily."

Mrs. Nickerson led the girls to a charming place about a quarter of a mile away. The house stood halfway between the river and the road. It was a two-story building with attractive, well-kept grounds.

"How lovely!" Nancy exclaimed.

"The owner, Mr. Webster," said Mrs. Nickerson, "has all kinds of unusual trees and shrubs on
the place besides an orange grove. He even has a
sausage tree. It is rarely seen in this country."

The visitors were intrigued by the wide variety
of trees and shrubs. Each had a plaque attached
that gave its Latin botanical name and the English
equivalent. Finally they came to the sausage tree.

It was about thirty feet tall with a profusion of
leaves. From the branches hung greenish sausage-
shaped fruit that resembled rough-textured melons. These were nearly six inches wide and twelve
inches long.

George felt one. "Wow! This would make a
real swinging weapon!" The others laughed.

Mrs. Nickerson said the fruit was not edible and
the pollen was carried in the spring from one
flower to another by bats.

"Ugh!" Bess exclaimed.

The tree was near a high wire-mesh fence which
looked strong enough to stop a large, fast-moving
truck.

Bess remarked, "That place next door sure is
spooky with all those old oak trees dripping with
Spanish moss. Who lives there?"

"I don't know," Mrs. Nickerson replied.

At that moment a chilling scream came from
inside the grounds!

CHAPTER IV

Newspaper Clue

THE piercing scream was not repeated. Nancy and her friends peered through the wire-mesh fence for a glimpse of a house. The jungle of trees with their long streamers of Spanish moss concealed whatever buildings might be on the property.

Nancy turned to Mrs. Nickerson. "Have you ever been in there?"

"No," Ned's mother replied. "The place is so forbidding I never tried to get acquainted with the occupants. Besides, I suspect whoever lives there owns some wild animals!"

George said she was curious to find out what she could. "If this fence doesn't go around the whole property, let's look for an opening and go in."

Bess objected at once. "Not me!"

Nancy settled the matter. "Actually we don't have time," she said. "Dad will be home, I'm sure, and I want to see if he has any news for us. But we'll come here the first chance we have."

Mrs. Nickerson teased, "Now I understand how you girls become involved in mysteries."

Nancy smiled. "Sometimes we do stumble upon them."

The group walked back to the Nickerson home, said good-by, and hurried to their boat. When they reached the Billington house, Mr. Drew was there. He was smiling and Nancy was sure he had had a successful morning.

"I like Mr. Datsun very much. It didn't take long to talk over the case," the lawyer said.

Mr. Drew delved into a breast pocket of his sports jacket and pulled out an envelope. "Surprise for you girls," he announced.

He handed the envelope to Nancy. She opened it and took out six badges on which the word PRESS was printed.

Mr. Drew explained, "As an accredited writer I was given badges at the news center for you and the boys to watch the moon shoot next week."

Bess and George stared at Mr. Drew. "You are an accredited writer?" Bess asked.

He chuckled and nodded. "I have a number of publications to my credit. Of course they're all on legal matters."

"How exciting!" said George. "Now we can see the lift-off and be as close as anyone is allowed."

"Right." Mr. Drew asked Hannah and the girls

if they would like to make a tour of the Kennedy Space Center that afternoon. All were enthusiastic and Nancy said, "It will give me a chance to get acquainted with the place where the explosive oranges were taken. I might pick up a clue."

As soon as luncheon was over they set off for the vast, well-kept government grounds that stretched along the ocean for miles. Mr. Drew parked the car near a sprawling building with a large roofed-over patio area. Under it were benches. Nancy and the others sat down to wait for a bus while her father bought tickets.

"This is the Visitor Information Center," Mr. Drew remarked when he came back.

Nancy was impressed by the large number of European and Asiatic tourists who were there.

"The Kennedy Space Center means a lot to the whole world," she thought, then walked up to the adjoining building to peer inside. There was a room with illuminated wall pictures of the various types of missiles. Here visitors could purchase books, postcards and souvenirs. Nancy saw an intriguing miniature model rocket. "I must come back and buy that," she decided.

"All aboard!" called George, and Nancy hurried to join the others.

The two-hour tour began, and the driver announced that they would cover fifty miles. Nancy and her friends were fascinated by the mock-ups of missiles and rockets stretching ahead of them in long rows. Most of them were in the familiar cone shape.

The guide said that the very first missile sent up from the Cape was a two-stage Bumper.

"The first stage was a captured German V-2 missile and the second an army WAC Corporal rocket. It was launched in July 1950."

Mr. Drew whispered to his daughter, "Our country has certainly come a long way in rocket building since then."

As the guide indicated gantries and rockets, Nancy recognized the names Thor, an early anti-ballistic missile, Titan, Minuteman and Saturn.

Next, the guide talked about the artificial satellites orbiting in space. He explained that the man-made moons are classified according to the jobs they do: (1) communication satellites, (2) weather satellites, (3) navigation satellites, (4) scientific satellites, and (5) military satellites.

"You, no doubt, are familiar with the Tiros and other satellites that take weather pictures and track hurricanes. Communication satellites, like Early Bird and Telstar, make it possible to send radio messages, telephone calls, and television programs from one continent to another in a matter of seconds."

The tour continued on to the moon rocket, which stood majestically next to its gantry. The onlookers craned their necks to see the top where the astronauts would live and work.

"It's all so overwhelming!" Hannah Gruen exclaimed.

The next stop on the tour was at the mammoth Vehicle Assembly Building. George remarked, "This is a real skyscraper."

"And it covers eight acres," the driver said. "The ceilings in the wings of this building are twenty stories high. That's where the smaller rockets are put together. The center section is fifty-two stories high. The big Saturns for trips to the moon and other planets are assembled in this area. Each booster for them is brought here on a very long covered barge which resembles an aluminum Quonset hut, painted white. The capsules come by truck or air."

When the sightseers walked inside to the Vehicle Assembly section they gasped. The center section was tall enough to accommodate a 360-foot rocket standing upright. Around the walls of the huge structure were metal scaffolds on which men had worked to complete the latest rocket assembly. From the ground floor those who were busy high above the visitors looked no larger than small boys.

"This is absolutely fascinating and unbelievable," Nancy said.

Suddenly she realized that Hannah Gruen was not with them. She looked at all the visitors but did not see the Drews' housekeeper.

"Maybe she stayed in the bus," Nancy thought,

and went outside to look. Hannah was not there.

"Where could she have gone?" Nancy asked herself, then told her father and the girls.

All of them searched but could not find Hannah. The guide was already calling to his passengers to board the bus.

"I don't want to leave without Hannah," Nancy said to her father. "This building is so huge if she started to walk around it, she couldn't possibly be back by this time."

Mr. Drew said he had an appointment with Commander Nichol at the Base in connection with the case. "Suppose I go ahead," he suggested, "and you girls keep on searching for Hannah. You can catch the next bus."

He spoke to the driver, who agreed that this would be all right.

Nancy, Bess, and George went back inside the big building and began looking again for Hannah. Moments later the door to an office opened. Hannah Gruen walked out, followed by a young man. They came directly to the three girls.

"This is Herb Baylor," Hannah said. "He's a distant relative of mine but I didn't know he was here. I happened to see him walk into an office and followed."

After the pleasant young man had acknowledged the introductions, Hannah went on, "Herb's an engineer and works on the assembling of rockets."

Nancy asked him, "Of course you know about the oranges containing the explosives that were sent into the Base."

"Yes, and I hear you're on Merritt Island to solve the mystery and clear Mr. Billington." He smiled boyishly. "I'll tell you a possible clue that I gave to Security."

"Wonderful!" Nancy replied. "What is it?"

Herb said he happened to be near the truck when it was leaving. "Part of a newspaper blew out. I picked it up and noticed a pencil-ringed personal. It was a garble of words that made no sense."

"What did it say?"

Herb replied, " *'Son on board ship ready to be sailor for peaceful kind of action.'* "

Nancy took a pad and pencil from her handbag and asked Herb to repeat the message. Quickly she read words numbered 1, 5, 9, and 13. The hidden message was, "Son ready for action."

She thanked Herb, telling him that the girls would work on it.

"I wish you luck," he said, smiling. "Now I must go back."

When the next bus came Nancy and her friends climbed aboard. The tour continued, and Nancy listened attentively to the driver's descriptions.

"On a long flight, like to the moon," the guide said, "an astronaut gets about twenty-eight hundred calories of food a day. Seventeen percent of this is protein, thirty-two percent fat, and fifty-one percent carbohydrates."

Bess gave a low giggle. "That's the place for me!"

The guide went on to say that the men eat four meals a day and a series of menus are rotated every four days. "All the food is in bars, cubes, and powders sealed in plastic pouches, or pastes which are kept in tubes."

Bess called out to the guide, "Could you tell us what some of the menus are?"

The man smiled. "Yes. How would you like this for breakfast? Strawberry cereal cubes, bacon squares, peanut-butter sandwiches, and orange juice."

"That's great," said Bess.

"Here's a typical dinner menu," the guide told her. "Beef with vegetables, spaghetti with meat sauce, toast squares, fruit cake made with dates, and tea."

"That would suit me," Bess commented. "It sounds yummy."

When the bus returned to the Visitor Information Center, Mr. Drew was waiting for them and they walked to the parking area.

As soon as they were seated in their car, George said, "Nancy, don't keep us in suspense any longer. What did you figure out of that newspaper clue?"

Nancy told her and the conversation turned to a series of guesses as to what it meant. They could only surmise that someone, somewhere, was ready to strike a blow. But who and at what?

When the group reached the house the Resardos were not there. Hannah remarked, "I suppose they won't show up until dinner is ready."

The girls offered to help her prepare dinner. When Nancy went into the dining room to set the table she noticed that a photograph of her father which he had sent Mr. Billington was gone from the buffet. She asked the others if any of them had placed it elsewhere. No one had.

"How strange!" said Hannah. She hurried into the living room and called out, "A picture of Mr. and Mrs. Billington is gone too."

On a hunch Nancy rushed upstairs to her father's room. A photograph of her with Bess and George, which he always took with him when he traveled, had been removed from the bureau. Next the young detective went to her own room and pulled out a dresser drawer. She had left a wallet in it containing a snapshot of her father and one of Ned Nickerson. They were missing. But none of the other contents had been taken.

Nancy dashed down the stairs. "Every photograph has been taken!" she exclaimed. "I'm sure they were stolen to use as identification of us because we're trying to solve the mystery of the explosive oranges!"

CHAPTER V

Alligator Attack

WHEN Bess heard about the missing photograph of Mr. Drew, she ran from the living room and up the stairs. Deep in her suitcase she had left a snapshot of herself with Nancy, George, Ned, Burt, and Dave. Bess riffled through the clothes still in the bag but could not find the picture.

"That was stolen too!" she told herself and hurried back downstairs to tell the others.

George said angrily, "Nobody has been in this house. We locked all the doors and windows before we left and they were still locked when we came home. I'm sure the Resardos took those pictures!"

Everyone agreed but Mr. Drew warned them that they had no evidence to prove this.

"Why don't we search their room?" George asked.

Before anybody could stop her, she bounded up

the stairway to the couple's quarters. But the Resardos' door was locked and continuous knocking on it brought no response. Dejected, George returned to the first floor.

"Now what do we do?" she asked Nancy.

"Suppose I phone the orange sorting and packing house. Antin may be there."

The worker who answered said that Antin had not been in all day. "He didn't tell us he wasn't coming, so we have no idea where he is."

Nancy thanked him and hung up. The Resardos returned just as the group was about to eat dinner.

"Where have you been all day?" George burst out.

Tina and Antin scowled but replied they had received word a relative in a distant city was ill and had gone to visit him. The couple turned toward the stove and picked up two dinner plates which were warming. As they helped themselves from each of the pots, Mr. Drew approached them.

"One minute," he said. "What can you tell us about all the photographs missing from the house?"

The Resardos looked at each other, then Antin said, "What are you talking about?"

When Mr. Drew explained, Antin declared he knew nothing about the pictures.

Tina spoke up. "I don't either. Are you accusing us of taking them?" She began to laugh raucously. "What would we want with photographs of you people?"

Mr. Drew turned on his heel and walked into the dining room. The Resardos filled two plates, got out some silver, and sat down at the kitchen table to eat.

The others were surprised that they had not gone upstairs. Nancy, however, figured the couple wanted to hear the conversation in the dining room. In a whisper she warned the rest not to discuss the Billington case. If the Resardos had hoped to pick up any information, they were disappointed. The talk was general, mostly about the fascinating trip through the Space Center.

When everyone finished eating, the Resardos piled their dirty dishes in the sink as usual, and went up to their room.

"I won't wash them!" Hannah Gruen said firmly.

Nancy smiled. "Tonight you're not washing anybody's dishes. You go into the living room and watch TV. Bess and George and I will take care of everything."

While the girls were doing this, Mr. Drew telephoned the police to report the theft of the photographs. Two officers came to the house. They agreed that it appeared to be an inside job and asked to talk with the Resardos. The couple vehemently declared their innocence. As the police were leaving, they told Mr. Drew that without any clues there was little hope of apprehending the thief.

Tina and Antin cast black looks at the others, then went upstairs without saying good night.

In the morning, when Nancy and her friends came downstairs, she found that the Resardos had already eaten breakfast and left the house. Their dirty dishes were piled up in the sink!

Hannah Gruen stared at the dried egg on the plates and the stained coffee cups in disgust. But she said nothing and started getting breakfast for the others.

When Mr. Drew came down, Nancy said, "Dad, I haven't had a chance to tell you about a darling house that's for sale." She described the Webster property.

He smiled at her enthusiasm. "I'll look at it," he said. "I can see you've fallen in love with the place."

While they were eating, a telephone call came for Mr. Drew. After a few minutes' conversation, he returned to the table and said he must leave for River Heights. "Something important has come up and I'll have to return home at once. Will you girls drive me to the airport?"

"Of course," Nancy replied. "Do you want me to call and see about planes?"

"If you will, please."

Nancy found out that if they left the house within ten minutes, her father could catch a nonstop flight to New York from Melbourne and get another plane to River Heights soon afterward. She hurried upstairs to tell her father and help him pack.

When Mr. Drew and the girls were ready to leave, he said to Hannah, "Take care. Better lock yourself in." The housekeeper nodded.

Two hours later the girls were ready to return from the Melbourne airport. Bess spoke up, "Let's take a scenic route home."

"All right," Nancy agreed. She consulted a road map and figured out what direction to take.

As they neared the area of the Cape, Bess spotted a long, wide ditch of water choked with water hyacinths, with bluish-violet lily-type blossoms.

"Oh I want to get some of those!" she said. "Please stop."

"They are pretty," Nancy agreed and pulled up to the side of the road.

Bess jumped from the car and went over to pick some of the blooms. After plucking several, she laid them at the edge of the water.

"Don't lean over so far or you'll fall in," George warned her cousin.

Bess rested on her heels and reached for another beautiful flower. Just as her hand touched it, something rustled among the leaves. The next moment an alligator thrust its snout from among the leaves and opened its jaws wide!

Bess screamed, jerked back, and sat down hard

on the muddy bank. The alligator moved toward her! Terrified, Bess scrambled up and ran to the car. The alligator disappeared under the water hyacinths. Nancy and George had hopped from the car to help her in. Bess was trembling and now began to sob.

"He—he was going to bite me!" the frightened girl exclaimed.

Nancy and George tried to calm her. In a few minutes Bess was all right but her white slacks were wet and muddy.

To take her mind off the unpleasant incident, Nancy said, "As soon as you change your clothes, Bess, let's go see the real-estate agent who is handling the sale of the Webster house. I want to look at the inside. After that we'll work on the explosive orange mystery."

"Good idea," said George. "Who is the realtor?"

"Mr. Scarlett."

When they reached the Billingtons', it did not take Bess long to change to dark-blue slacks and a clean shirt. After a quick lunch the girls set off again. They drove directly to Mr. Scarlett's office. Nancy parked and they walked up to the one-story building, then stopped short. A sign tacked to the door read:

CLOSED FOR VACATION
WILL OPEN IN TWO WEEKS

The alligator moved toward Bess

"We can't stay that long!" said Bess.

"I know," Nancy agreed. "Wait here, girls."

She went to a nearby store and asked where Mr. Scarlett lived. She hoped the realtor was not out of town.

"He didn't tell me his plans," said the storekeeper, and gave her the address of Mr. and Mrs. Scarlett.

When the girls rang his doorbell, there was no answer. Windows were closed and blinds were down.

"Maybe they're only away for the day," George said optimistically.

Nancy was determined to see the inside of the Webster house and told herself, "I'll find a way!"

George remarked, "Normally a realtor wouldn't go away without making provisions for prospective buyers to see properties he has listed."

On the way back to the Billington house, Bess gave a tremendous sigh. "Can't we relax and play some tennis?" she asked. "Then we'll go sleuthing."

"Great idea!" said George. "I'll take on both of you."

Bess giggled. "How we hate ourselves," she teased. "Just for that, I accept. Nancy and I will whitewash you! Three love sets in a row!"

Bess came near being right. She and Nancy won the first two games. By the time the girls had finished three sets, the scores stood two sets for Nancy and Bess and one for George.

"I'll get even another time!" George vowed with a wide grin.

As they walked from the court, the cousins asked Nancy what was next on the schedule.

"You're so good at keeping your mind on two things at once," said Bess, "that half your brain was playing tennis and the other half conjuring up something."

Nancy laughed. "I was just thinking that if I call Dad's friend Commander Nichol at the Base he'll give me the name of the guard who admitted the driver with the explosive oranges."

"And after that—" George prodded her.

"After that," Nancy replied, "we'll try to talk to that man."

Commander Nichol said that the guard's name was Patrick Croft.

"He has been dismissed," the commander went on, "but hasn't left town. He's at home," and gave Nancy the address.

After she had said good-by, Nancy turned to the girls. "Let's go! Maybe by talking to Mr. Croft we can get a clue to the man who impersonated Mr. Billington and drove into the Base."

CHAPTER VI

Exciting Evening

PATRICK Croft lived alone in a small house. When Nancy explained why the girls had come, he invited them inside. Before he sat down the sad-looking man offered them some candy he had made. They learned he was a bachelor and liked to cook. Nancy surmised that Mr. Croft was reserved and not apt to defend himself when any trouble arose.

"That's too bad," the young detective told herself. "Maybe if Croft had been more aggressive, he wouldn't have been dismissed from NASA."

When Nancy queried him about the driver of the truck with the explosive oranges, Croft described him minutely.

At once Nancy thought, "It is true then that this man could have passed as Mr. Billington!"

Croft went on, "The driver said he was Mr. Billington, whom I don't know. He had all the proper credentials with him, so of course I let him in. The last I saw of him he was turning toward the food supply depot and I assumed that was where he went."

"And he didn't?" George asked.

Mr. Croft smiled. "A guard got aboard and took him there. Fortunately the explosive oranges were discovered before any damage was done. But it's my opinion he intended to blow up part of the rocket while it was still in the Vehicle Assembly Building.

"I'm mighty sorry about the whole thing, but I don't think I should have been dismissed. The explosives had been put in the oranges very cleverly and they looked innocent enough in the sacks.

"I hope someday I'll be reinstated." Mr. Croft heaved a great sigh. "By the way, I was taken to identify Mr. Billington. He and the impostor look enough alike to be twins."

The girls felt sorry for Croft. They realized his dismissal had been necessary. After the saboteur was caught, perhaps Croft would be exonerated.

Nancy told him that her father was the lawyer who had been retained to defend Mr. Billington, but that he in turn had engaged the services of Johnson Datsun.

Croft said he had heard of Mr. Datsun. "He's a very fine lawyer. If anybody can straighten out this case, I'm sure he can."

"But it's not just a legal matter," Bess spoke up. "It's a mystery too. Nancy's an amateur detective and—"

Nancy smiled. "And with the help of my two good friends here, I have solved some mysteries."

Mr. Croft's eyes opened wide. "That's wonderful," he said. "I always wanted to be a detective, but I wasn't cut out for that kind of work. The nearest I came to it was checking people's credentials when they entered the Space Center." He sighed again.

Nancy stood up. Bess and George took the cue from her and arose also.

"Mr. Croft," said Nancy, "if you should hear or recall anything that might help us solve this mystery, will you telephone me?"

"I'll be glad to," the man replied. Nancy gave him the Billingtons' address and telephone number, then the girls left.

Upon reaching home, they found Hannah Gruen quite excited. George asked, "Have the Resardos pulled another fast one?"

"No," the housekeeper replied. "I haven't seen them all day. But I think I've picked up a clue for you. If I'm right, it may spell trouble or danger for you, Nancy, and your father."

"What do you mean?" Nancy queried.

Hannah produced the day's newspaper. She pointed out a personal. It read:

"Dorothy's son has just released trunk. It is empty. Advise at once where to find contents."

Immediately the three girls read words numbered 1, 5, 9, 13. These said, "Dorothy's released empty where."

Bess said, "They don't make sense."

Hannah was eager to tell her clue. "But put the first letters of those words together," she said. "They spell Drew."

"Wow!" George exclaimed. "What could this possibly mean?"

Nancy did not answer. She had not yet figured out the meaning of the personal but one thing was certain—someone was sending a message which could have dire consequences for her and her father and possibly her friends. She was worried but did not speak her thoughts aloud.

Bess admitted that she was scared. "I think we'd better give up our sleuthing and leave here," she declared.

George said, "Bess, you know as well as I do that the thrust of a hundred-thousand-pound rocket couldn't force Nancy to give up this case."

Nancy smiled. "A wild thought just occurred to me. Suppose this reference to Drew has something to do with our interest in the Webster house. We already know that Mr. Scarlett has gone on vacation. For some reason unknown to us, the people who use the code may not want us here and encouraged Scarlett to go away. What we must do is find out that reason."

Hannah Gruen reminded the girls that their dinner was ready. "The meal will be spoiled if you don't eat it now."

Nancy, Bess, and George washed their hands and combed their hair, then sat down at the table with Hannah. All had good appetites and thoroughly enjoyed the delicious roast beef. They were tidying up the kitchen when Bess remarked, "The Resardos missed a good dinner, but we certainly didn't miss them."

"Maybe they're not coming back at all!" George said with a grin. "It would please me if I never saw that couple again."

"I agree with you," said Mrs. Gruen.

That evening the phone was kept busy. First Nancy called her father and told him all she had learned that day.

After hearing the whole story, he observed, "It's evident that someone or a group is keeping an eye on us. The situation could become dangerous."

"But you're not going to let them scare us away, are you?" Nancy asked.

She was sure her father was going to say no and he did not disappoint her. He warned Nancy, however, to keep alert for trouble.

"I'll get back there as quickly as I can," he added.

Nancy had just put down the phone when it

rang. The voice at the other end said, "Well, I'm glad I got you at last. I've been trying for hours to get hold of you."

"Hi, Ned!" Nancy said. "We can hardly wait for the house party to start, but we haven't been idle. There'll be lots to tell when you boys arrive."

"No doubt," Ned said. "I've never known a time when you weren't doing as much as three people. I have just one favor to ask—that you have this mystery solved before Burt and Dave and I arrive. We want to have fun."

"Why, Ned," said Nancy, a teasing tone in her voice, "I thought you adored solving mysteries and tracking down villains."

Ned laughed. "You're right. Okay, Nancy," he added, "I'll help bring this mystery to a quick termination!"

"Actually there are two mysteries," said Nancy. "The explosive oranges and the spooky-looking grounds of an estate on this island. When I get a chance I'm going to investigate the place."

"I'll take the spooky one," Ned answered.

Nancy laughed. "I hope to have at least one of them solved before you arrive."

Ned chuckled, then became serious. "Watch your step. I don't want anything to happen to you."

After he and Nancy had said good night, she joined the other girls. Within seconds there was another call.

"Maybe it's Burt," George spoke up.

"And maybe you're both wrong," Hannah remarked. "The call might be for me—from Herb. He said he'd phone and make a date to call on us. I think he was very much impressed with you three girls."

As Hannah had predicted, the caller was Herb, who told her he had been put on special assignment. "I won't be able to come over to the Billington house until after the lift-off."

"By that time we'll probably be gone," Hannah said, "but give us a ring anyway."

The girls were giggling when Hannah returned. Bess teased her. "Did Herb want to make a date to take you up in a rocket?"

The housekeeper flushed slightly but joined in the banter. "Don't think I didn't catch on. He wanted to see you girls!"

Just then the phone rang again. Burt and Dave were calling. Both boys were eagerly looking forward to the house party at the Nickersons' and sent their best wishes to Hannah and Nancy.

By bedtime the Resardos still had not returned and everyone wondered if the couple would put in an appearance.

As the group was about to go upstairs the telephone rang again. Nancy, nearest the instrument, answered.

"Is this Nancy Drew?" a man asked.

"Yes."

"This is Patrick Croft. I've been trying to call you but your line has been busy. A man phoned me around eight o'clock. He sounded like the driver I let into the Base with the oranges. He told me I was to have nothing more to do with Nancy Drew or I'd be harmed."

"That's dreadful!" Nancy said.

The words were barely out of her mouth when Patrick Croft gave a cry of panic. "Someone's breaking in!" he shouted. "Help! Help!"

CHAPTER VII

False Information

THE phone connection remained on but there were no voices. Evidently Patrick Croft had run away from the instrument without hanging it up. Nancy could hear banging and shouting, then a crash, as if the intruder had broken open the door.

Nancy hung up, waited a few minutes for the connection to be broken, then called police headquarters. She told the sergeant on duty what had happened at Croft's house. He assured her that two officers would be sent there immediately.

Nancy rushed upstairs to tell Hannah and the girls of Croft's predicament. "I'm going over to see what happened!"

"Not by yourself," Hannah spoke up firmly. "We'll all go. This is shocking. Poor Mr. Croft!"

With Nancy at the wheel, they covered the distance to his house in a short time. A police car and an ambulance stood in front and sympathetic neighbors had begun to gather.

"Oh, he's been hurt!" Bess exclaimed.

Nancy pulled up to the curb and jumped out. Patrick Croft was just being brought out on a stretcher. He was unconscious and his face the color of pale alabaster.

Two policemen followed. After the ambulance pulled away, Nancy spoke to the taller officer, telling him she was the person who had phoned headquarters.

"I'd like to explain to you in more detail what I know about the attack tonight."

"Come with me, miss," said the officer, and added, "My name is Regan."

He led the way back into the house, then took a notebook and pencil from a pocket. "Tell me everything you can," he said. "Sometimes a small detail that the average person considers unimportant can prove to be a valuable clue."

Nancy knew this very well from her own sleuthing experiences. She introduced herself and told where she was from, then said, "Mr. Croft was a security guard at NASA. He's the one responsible for allowing the truck with explosive oranges to come onto the Base."

"Oh you know about that," the officer replied.

Nancy nodded, then related Patrick Croft's telephone conversation verbatim.

"So Croft thought the caller might have been the truck driver," Officer Regan observed. "If he wasn't Mr. Billington, have you any idea who he is? And why did the person who phoned not want Croft to contact you?"

"I don't know the man's name," Nancy answered. "That's what I'm in Florida to find out. My father and a local lawyer are trying to solve this case and prove Mr. Billington innocent."

"I see," the policeman said. "Poor Croft was beaten into unconsciousness so it will be some time before he'll be able to answer any of our questions."

Regan told her that there was only one set of clear footprints but this was not a help in identification because the intruder had worn flippers.

"Also, the man must have had on gloves," the officer said, "because he left no fingerprints."

The word flippers caught Nancy's attention and she remarked, "The man you'll be looking for could be a snorkeler."

"You're right," Regan admitted. Then he asked, "By the way, have you and your friends visited the Real Eight Museum of Sunken Treasure yet?"

"No, we haven't."

"Do by all means. It's most interesting, even though a little terrifying if you visualize what happened during one of the worst hurricanes on record. Well," the officer said, "I must go. Thank you for your information."

He escorted Nancy outside. His fellow officer produced a padlock for the broken front door and pocketed the key. The police car pulled away. A curious group of neighbors who had gathered finally dispersed.

Hannah and the girls started home. On the way Nancy said she felt largely responsible for what had happened to Croft.

Hannah asked, "How could you possibly be responsible?"

Nancy replied, "We know there are people who don't want us working on Mr. Billington's case. They're probably watching all our movements. They found out I went to Croft's house today and figured he had told me all he knew about the case. That's why he was beaten up!"

"How terrible!" Bess said angrily.

"Here's another possibility," said George. "Suppose Croft is actually one of the gang? He might have been the inside man."

Hannah spoke up. "If Croft is one of the gang, why would they beat him up?"

"Because," George replied, "he was given a job to do at the Base and he bungled it."

Nancy remarked, "That's good reasoning, George. I don't happen to agree with it, though. I think Croft was given the beating to keep him from saying any more. He may suspect other people whom he didn't tell us about."

When she turned into the Billingtons' driveway, George said, "The Resardos' car is here."

"That Antin is a cheat!" Hannah burst out. "Mr. Billington pays him for working in the grove and taking care of these grounds. He hasn't touched the lawn or garden since we came. The grass is getting so brown I put on the sprinkler today."

The housekeeper unlocked the rear door and turned on the light. "How about a little ice cream before we go to bed?" She went to the refrigerator to take some out.

Nancy glanced at her watch. It was after eleven o'clock. "I wonder if it's too late to call Mr. Datsun," she said to the others. "I think I should tell him what happened tonight."

Hannah, Bess, and George agreed, so Nancy went to the phone and picked it up. Someone was using it!

As the young detective listened, a man said, "Got it straight? R-day."

George had followed Nancy to the hall. Nancy made motions indicating that her friend was to run upstairs and see who was on the extension phone.

As George took the steps two at a time, Nancy heard a man's muffled reply, "Okay." The connection was cut off.

George came down the stairs to report that she had found no one using the extension phone up there.

"The call must have been made from the orange packing house," Nancy declared.

Hannah had come to see what was troubling Nancy. After hearing about the conversation, she said firmly, "Nancy, you're not going to that place to find out. It's too dangerous. Anyway, the person who used the phone has probably left by this time."

Nancy agreed. "But I think Antin should investigate," she said. "I'm going upstairs and tell him."

George gave a sardonic laugh. "He won't thank you for waking him up."

"I don't care," Nancy replied, and mounted the stairway. She knocked on the Resardos' door. There was no response, but after a second knock, a woman's sleepy voice said, "Who's there?"

"It's Nancy Drew, Tina. I'd like to speak to Antin. It's very important."

There was a long pause, then finally Tina came to the door. "Antin can't see you now. He's taking a bath."

"Please tell him that some prowler is in the packing house. He'd better go find out about him."

"Okay, I'll tell him."

Nancy returned to the first floor. She and the others ate their ice cream, but Antin Resardo did not appear.

"Some more of his indifference," George remarked. "He's a surly person."

"Yes," Bess spoke up. "He's no help at all around here. I certainly think Mr. Billington should be told."

"You can bet he will be," Hannah informed her.

When they finished the ice cream, the girls washed and dried the dishes and spoons. Then they put out the lights and followed Hannah up the stairway. Suddenly Nancy turned back.

"What is it?" Bess asked her.

"Listen!" said Nancy. "I think someone is using a key to open the kitchen door."

Led by Nancy, the group tiptoed down the stairway and went toward the kitchen. The rear door opened just as Nancy clicked on the overhead light. They were astounded to see Antin Resardo coming in.

"You weren't taking a bath at all as Tina said!" George cried out. "You were in the orange packing house phoning!"

Nancy walked up to him. "What does R-day mean?" she demanded.

Antin gave a start, then suddenly his face flushed with anger and he glared at the young detective.

"You little sneak!" he yelled.

The next second he grabbed her by the shoulders and shook her so hard Nancy felt as if her head would snap off.

CHAPTER VIII

Doubting Workmen

"Stop that!" George yelled at Antin.

She grabbed his arm and as Nancy staggered away, George buckled the man's knees and flipped him over her shoulder. He fell to the floor with a crash.

"Good for you, George!" exclaimed Bess in glee.

Antin had been taken completely by surprise and had had the wind knocked out of him. Slowly he arose.

Meanwhile Hannah had rushed to Nancy's side and asked, "Are you all right? That was a contemptible thing to do to you!" she said. "Antin, hereafter don't you ever dare lay a finger on Nancy or any of the rest of us!"

Nancy assured Hannah she would be her normal self in a few minutes and flopped into a chair. Antin looked at her, then said grudgingly, "I didn't mean to hurt you. I'm sorry if I did. You make me see red when you act suspicious of me. You mentioned my taking a bath. By the time I finished, Tina was asleep.

"It worried me that since I'd been away all day the machinery might not have been switched off in the packing house. I went to investigate.

"While there, I decided to put in a phone call to a friend of mine who is giving a surprise birthday party for his wife. Her name is Ruth. We are calling it R-day."

The commotion had brought Tina downstairs in her robe and slippers. She looked at the group questioningly. Antin repeated his story about R-day to her and she nodded affirmation.

Hannah spoke up. "There may have been misunderstanding on all sides. Why don't we talk this whole thing out?"

"Good idea," said Antin.

Mrs. Gruen went on, "In the first place, I may as well tell you I resent your not helping in the house. You eat the food I cook and even leave your dirty dishes for me to wash."

Tina retorted, "Mr. Billington didn't tell me I had to wait on these extra people. He just told me Mr. Drew and his daughter might be down. I'm not strong and I'm not too well," she went on, "and I won't wait on so many people! That's final!"

"She's right," Antin burst out. "Between all the extra work and you people practically accusing us of being crooks, I think Tina and I will move to a motel until after you go home."

Hannah and the girls looked at one another. It would be a great relief to have the unpleasant Resardos out of the house. But if the couple stayed, they could be kept under surveillance.

Antin went on, "You think I had something to do with those explosive oranges. Well I didn't, and I gave the FBI an airtight alibi about where I was the day it happened."

Nancy did not like the man's defensive attitude. She knew that guilty people often play the part of aggrieved persons, trying to cover up the truth. Was this the case with the Resardos?

Again Hannah spoke up. "I'm glad we had this talk," she said. "Tina and Antin, I'm sure Mr. Billington would be very hurt if you leave and he might even decide not to let you come back."

This thought startled the couple. They looked at each other and finally Tina said, "All right, we'll stay. I'll help with the cooking whenever Antin and I are here. I guess all of us can keep the house clean."

Nancy sensed the Resardos were annoyed because Hannah had won her point. The couple wished the others good night and went to their room. George looked after them. Did she imagine it, or was Antin limping a little because of her Judo trick?

The atmosphere the next morning was a bit

strained, but Tina did help prepare breakfast. She did not serve the food, however. Instead she and Antin sat down in the kitchen to eat, while the others carried their plates of eggs and bacon to the dining room.

Immediately after breakfast Nancy and Bess went upstairs to make their beds. George was about to follow a few minutes later when she saw Antin leave the house. On a hunch she trailed him, keeping well out of sight.

The foreman went directly to the packing house and George started back through the grove. Suddenly it occurred to her that she might get a clue to the orange mystery from some of the pickers. Seeing two of them a little distance away, she walked toward the men.

When George came near, she heard one man say, "I wouldn't trust that guy any place."

His companion replied, "Me neither."

The other man said laughingly, "I'll bet you the boss is making a killing for himself!" Were they talking about Antin or Mr. Billington?

Puzzled but suspicious, George hurried back to the house. By the time she arrived Tina had gone upstairs and Bess and Nancy had come down. George told them what she had heard in the grove.

"Which boss do you think the men were talking about?" she asked.

Nancy smiled. "I'll try to find out."

She went to the phone and called the packing

house. When a man answered, she said, "I'd like to speak to the boss."

"Okay. I'll call him," the worker replied. He yelled. "Antin, you're wanted on the phone."

Noiselessly Nancy put down the receiver and reported to the other girls.

"Shall we go tackle him?" George asked. "I'm sure he's doublecrossing Mr. Billington."

Nancy agreed but said, "I have a feeling that today Antin will be on his good behavior. In the meantime let's try once more to get into the Webster house. I can't wait to see the inside."

"How are you going to accomplish that without a key?" Bess queried.

Nancy said she would start by going back to Mr. Scarlett's office. She might be able to learn something from nearby store owners.

When the girls reached the realtor's office, they were surprised to see the door open. Lovely, low singing was coming from within. Wondering what was going on, the three callers walked inside. A stout, pretty woman was singing a lullaby as she dusted the furniture.

Upon seeing the girls she smiled broadly and said, "You want Mr. Scarlett?"

"Yes we do," Nancy replied.

The pleasant woman jerked her thumb toward a closed door. "He's in there."

Nancy was surprised and delighted. Now she could get the key!

She knocked on the closed door. A voice said, "Come in!"

As Nancy walked in, she said, "Good morning. I'm Nancy Drew."

"Oh yes. Mrs. Nickerson left a note you might come. Why did you?"

"To have you show me the interior of the Webster house," she answered.

The realtor scowled. "Don't you know I'm on vacation?"

"Your sign said so, but you seem to be right here," the young detective replied with a smile.

"Well, I am on vacation. There were certain papers in my files I had to pick up."

Nancy pretended not to notice he was trying to evade her. She said pleasantly, "I'm lucky to have found you. If you can't show me and my friends the Webster house, then, since you know the Nickersons, will you please lend me the key? I'll return it through your mail slot, unless my father decides he wants to buy the place. In that case I'll keep the key."

"You'll do nothing of the sort," Mr. Scarlett said unpleasantly. "The house is not for you. You wouldn't like it and there are lots of things the matter with the place."

"Like what?" Nancy asked.

Mr. Scarlett frowned. "It's not necessary for me to go into that."

Nancy was not ready to give up yet. She smiled.

"Why are you so anxious to keep us away from the Webster property? If I were a suspicious person, I would think something wrong was going on there."

Mr. Scarlett's eyes narrowed angrily. "Nonsense."

"Then why are you refusing to let me see it?"

Mr. Scarlett bit his lip. "Oh, all right," he said. "I don't have time to show you the place myself." He opened the drawer and took out a key with the letter W cut into it. A tag marked Webster was attached. "Here you are," he said icily. "But if anything is missing or disturbed, you'll be held responsible."

"I understand," Nancy said.

She took the key and joined Bess and George. They said good-by to the cleaning woman and went out to the car. Nancy drove directly to the lovely house on the Indian River and the three girls went in.

"How wonderful!" Bess exclaimed, after looking around. "It's even nicer inside than outside."

Nancy too was charmed by the place, which was attractively furnished. The walls of the modern Spanish-type rooms were artistically decorated. In this warm climate the whole place had an air of coolness and true hospitality.

"I don't see anything the matter with this house," said George. "Mr. Scarlett's opinion is for the birds." The others agreed and all of them wondered why the realtor had tried to discourage them.

Suddenly they were startled by the same chilling scream they had heard when looking over the grounds with Mrs. Nickerson.

"There it is again!" Bess murmured. "Ugh! I wouldn't want to live here with that gross thing next door."

"Let's find out what it is!" Nancy urged.

"Not me," Bess said firmly.

"Don't be chicken," George chided her cousin.

Reluctantly Bess went outside and Nancy locked the door. The girls hurried toward the heavy wire-mesh fence. There was another scream, followed by a snarl.

"It's a wild animal!" Bess whispered. "We'd better run!"

CHAPTER IX

Jungle Threat

"No, Bess," said Nancy. "If Dad decides to buy this place, we must know what's going on next door. And I plan to find out right now. Let's walk along the shore and investigate."

Though Bess was fearful, she followed the others along the fence. It ran onto a peninsula beyond the Webster property. At the riverfront the fence turned left abruptly.

There was no bulkhead along the water and the earth was muddy and slippery. After a few steps Nancy, Bess, and George decided to take off their shoes and carry them. They rolled up their slacks knee-length and started across the swampy ground.

"Watch your step!" Bess warned. "No telling what we might step on—a lizard, snake or—Oh!"

She lost her balance but managed after a few gyrations with her arms to right herself. "I knew I shouldn't have come," she complained.

Moments later the girls reached the corner of the steel-mesh fence near the far side of the peninsula. It turned left again. The three trekked alongside through the mass of trees and bushes. They found it helpful to use the steel wire for support.

The girls had not gone far before they realized this was a real jungle. Going barelegged and barefoot did not seem safe, so the three friends put their shoes back on and rolled down their slacks.

"When will we get to the end of this?" Bess asked impatiently. Nancy said she judged it could not be much farther to the street.

The next moment the girls stood stock-still. From inside the grounds had come a loud roar.

"That's a lion!" George exclaimed. "Maybe this is a zoo."

Nancy said it was certainly not a public one.

"If it were," she surmised, "I'm sure Mrs. Nickerson would have known about it and told us. Besides, we'd have seen signs posted."

She and George pushed ahead, with Bess at their heels, terror-stricken. She suddenly gave a cry and pointed inside the fence.

A group of large African animals was galloping among the trees toward the girls. Roars, growls, and hisses filled the air. The big beasts, having scented the newcomers, pawed and clamored at the fence to get at them. A huge black leopard eyed the intruders, then began to climb the steel mesh.

Bess screamed and cried, "Look out, George!" Her cousin stood by the fence, fascinated, as Bess ran.

Nancy backed away quickly, but through the moss-draped oaks she could see a powerful-looking man running toward them, snapping a long whip.

The cracking of it finally had an effect on the animals. All of them slunk back except the leopard. He had almost reached the top of the fence and might spring over at any second!

"Get down!" the man thundered at him.

He wore a khaki suit and helmet like those used on African safaris. Now he swung the whip against the fence. It made a ringing sound and vibrated the wire mesh.

The leopard looked at his keeper balefully, then slowly climbed down. The man kept cracking the whip in the air and against the ground until all the animals loped off among the trees.

Their master turned his attention to the girls. He asked angrily, "What are you doing here?"

"Just looking," Nancy replied.

The man stared hard at each one of them before speaking again. "I guess I don't have to tell you this is a dangerous place. Stay away!"

From a little distance Bess called back, "You bet we will."

George said nothing, but Nancy asked, "Why do you have such dangerous animals here?"

"I train them and sell them to a circus."

The young detective was surprised to hear this. She knew that few circuses own the animals which are shown. They belong to the trainers who perform with them.

"What circus do you sell them to?" she queried.

Once more the big man stared at the girl until his eyes were only slits. Finally he opened them wide and said, "Tripp Brothers."

"Thank you," said Nancy. "How do we get to the main road from here? Follow this fence?"

The trainer replied shortly, "Go back the way you came."

Nancy would have preferred walking alongside the enclosure all the way to the street, but the man stood watching.

After they had traversed the full distance to where the fence turned, Nancy looked over her shoulder. The trainer was gone. She said eagerly, "Let's turn around and follow this side to find out what we can."

"Oh please don't!" Bess begged. "Those animals may come after us again and the leopard jump over the fence!"

"I'm willing to take the chance. George, are you?" Nancy asked.

"Sure thing."

Nancy took the key to the Webster house from her pocket. "Bess," she said, "if you don't want to come with us, why don't you go on and wait in the house?"

"Look out, George!" Bess cried out

Bess could see that there was no talking Nancy and George out of learning more about the jungle-like property. With a great sigh she said, "Oh, all right. I'll tag along. But if anything happens, don't say I didn't warn you."

The girls began their trek up the peninsula through the woods, following the fence. A distance ahead it suddenly turned to the left.

"The fence ends at a house!" Nancy whispered.

She and the others approached carefully and stared at the building. It was a very old mansion but large and well preserved. The walls were covered almost entirely with clinging vines and green moss. Great oak trees with long streamers of Spanish moss surrounded it, giving a weird and forbidding effect.

"A real spook house!" Bess said in a low voice. "Well, Nancy, have you seen enough? Let's go!"

Nancy inched closer to the wire fence and peered through. She could see several large cages attached to the rear of the house. The animals that had tried to attack the girls were now in them and sleeping. At the moment the breeze was blowing toward the girls, and the animals could not pick up their scent.

Bess tugged at Nancy's arm. "Let's not tempt fate," she begged. "Please come on."

Nancy could feel Bess trembling and nodded in agreement.

Nancy wondered how far it was to the street.

There seemed to be no road leading out, but she concluded there must be some way for cars and people to get in and out of the grounds.

Presently she spotted a truck off to one side. There was no name on it but she jotted down the license number.

"Here's what I've been looking for," she whispered, and pointed to a narrow road which zigzagged among the moss-covered trees.

As the girls walked along it silently, they listened for sounds of anyone approaching and watched the ground to avoid any holes. George, however, sank down in a soft spot. Her feet were sucked in so quickly she could not pull them out.

After trying for several moments she called out, "Girls, come and help me! I'm stuck!"

It took the combined efforts of Nancy and Bess to pull George out of the oozy mass. She looked down at her shoes which had changed from white to brown.

"I'm sure a mess!" she said. "The sooner I can get into a tub the better I'll like it." She thanked her rescuers who could not help laughing at George's appearance. Mud was splattered over her clothes, hair, and face.

A few feet farther on, the ground was harder and the girls quickened their pace. As they zigzagged along the curving road, the three grew careless about being watchful.

Nancy suddenly pulled back and bumped

against George. The others looked to see what had startled her. A snake had begun to unwind itself from a tree branch and was trying to reach Nancy with its forked tongue!

She recovered her wits quickly and said, "He won't harm us if we don't bother him."

"I hope you're right," said Bess, and took a circuitous route to avoid the reptile.

In a few moments the girls came to a small orange grove. As they hurried through it, Bess picked one of the luscious-looking fruit and put it into her pocket.

"In case I get hungry," she explained to the others.

A few minutes later the girls reached another bit of jungle-like area. If it had not been for the roadway, they would have found it hard going through stout reeds and brier bushes. At last the street came into sight.

Nancy, in the lead, suddenly called back in a whisper, "Hide!"

CHAPTER X

Disastrous Fire

"QUICK!" said Nancy, ducking behind a brier bush. "Mr. Scarlett is just outside in a car!"

Bess and George squatted down too. The three remained very still, not making a sound.

Mr. Scarlett got out of his car and walked up and down, looking and listening. The girls were puzzled by his actions. Perhaps someone had seen them going toward the moss-covered mansion and had reported this to him.

In a few minutes the realtor seemed satisfied about something. He got back into his car. Then, to the girls' amazement, he drove toward them along the winding path. They crouched lower behind the tall bushes. His car soon disappeared but they could hear the motor. Seconds later it was shut off approximately where the house would be.

"He must know the animal trainer," Nancy thought.

She and her friends came from hiding. Nancy wanted to go back to the moss-covered mansion but Bess objected. "I think we've had enough adventures for one day. Besides, George is a mess. Please, let's return to the Billingtons."

As they walked down the street toward the Webster house to get their car, the girls discussed Scarlett's furtive behavior. Why had he come to the mansion with the wild-animal enclosure?

"He's hiding something, that's sure," George declared. "Nancy, if you see him again, are you going to ask him why he was here?"

"No, George. I believe we can find out more by having him think we didn't see him."

When they reached home Hannah Gruen met them at the kitchen door. "My word, George, where have you been?" she cried out. "Did you fall in the water?"

"I wish I had," said George. "I'd have been better off." Quickly she explained about their sleuthing trip to the moss-covered mansion.

The housekeeper was aghast. "The place sounds dreadful. You had better not go there again."

Bess said, "You can bet I'm not going to."

She pulled the orange from her pocket, and told Hannah she had taken it from a tree at the strange house.

"This isn't the same kind as Mr. Billington's,"

Bess said. "Do you suppose it's a Hamlin, the same as the oranges that were delivered to the Space Center?"

The thought intrigued Nancy. On a bookshelf she had noticed a volume marked *Oranges* and went to get it. The book was filled with color pictures and one by one she compared Bess's orange with those in the book.

"This is not a Valencia," she said, "because it's the wrong time of year for that kind of tree to be bearing. The fruit's ripe in the spring. Mr. Billington's, as you know, are Pineapple Oranges. Remember their bright-orange skin and pineappley shape?" Nancy turned the page and exclaimed, "Here it is! The oranges at the moss-covered mansion are not Hamlins but Parson Browns. Hamlins have a smooth skin while the Parson Browns are pebbly-skinned."

George sighed. "I guess we'll have to ride around looking for Hamlin groves to see if we can pick up any clue to the ones that were brought into the Space Center."

The girls decided to start their search directly after luncheon. They hurried upstairs to take baths and put on fresh clothes.

By the time they came down again, Tina was in the kitchen helping Hannah. The three girls winked at one another and began to set the table.

The menu called for baked chicken with a special kind of cream sauce. Tina said she had never heard of it and did not know how to make the sauce.

"Nancy does it very well," Hannah said proudly, and called, "Nancy dear, will you come and make cream sauce for the chicken?"

Smiling, Nancy hurried to the kitchen and prepared it.

When everything was ready, Hannah and the girls went to the dining room. They invited Tina to eat with them, but the woman refused, saying she was not hungry. Perhaps by the time Antin came in, she would be ready for her lunch.

Instinct told Nancy not to talk about the moss-covered mansion within Tina's hearing. The group were relieved when she went outdoors and walked into the grove.

The telephone rang. Nancy answered it. Mr. Datsun, the lawyer, was calling. He wanted to know if Nancy had anything to report. She gave a quick account of her sleuthing but admitted she had learned little about the explosive oranges.

"No one has been able to track down any clue except to Mr. Billington," the lawyer said.

On a hunch Nancy told him about the old mansion. "Do you know who lives there?"

"No," the lawyer replied. "Why?"

Nancy explained about the possibility of her father buying the Webster place and the strange behavior of Mr. Scarlett. "Are you acquainted with him?"

"I know there's a realtor of that name," said Mr. Datsun, "but I can't tell you anything about him. I'm afraid I'm no help to you, but I'm hoping you can help me.

"Nancy, a very odd note was left under my office door. Maybe you can figure it out. This is what it says:

" *'Can a mouse with a brain of jelly capture a lion with nerves of steel?'* "

"How strange!" Nancy remarked. "Would you mind repeating it?"

Mr. Datsun read it again and Nancy quickly wrote down the words and read those numbered 1, 5, 9, 13. Neither the words nor the first letters of them made any sense.

"Are you still there?" Mr. Datsun asked.

"I'm sorry," said Nancy. "I was trying to see if there might be a code in this message. I think not. But it occurs to me that it could have been written by some sarcastic person interested in the case of the explosive oranges. The message might imply that you and my father are as helpless as a mouse against a lion."

"That's a very good guess," the lawyer remarked.

Nancy went on, "Whoever the lion is, we'll catch him!"

"Indeed we will!" Mr. Datson agreed.

After the conversation ended, Nancy continued to think about the message. She suddenly remembered the lion at the moss-covered mansion. Suppose that by some chance this was the beast referred to in the mysterious note! It could mean that the strange setup of the animal enclosure and the odd behavior of Mr. Scarlett are connected with the explosive oranges!

"It would explain why the girls and I aren't wanted at the Webster house," Nancy told herself.

At this moment Bess came to warn her that Antin and Tina had come in. The caretaker was taciturn. Not only did he not speak to anyone but did not wait to eat lunch. Instead, the couple went up to their room.

"What's the matter with him?" George asked.

Before anyone could hazard a guess, an alarm bell began to ring.

"What's that for?" George asked.

There was pounding on the stairway and Antin came rushing down. "Fire!" he shouted, and rushed out the rear door.

Everyone followed. He sped through the grove to the packing house.

Suddenly Nancy stopped. "I wonder if anyone notified the fire department," she said. "I'd better go back and phone them anyway."

"I'll go with you," said Bess. "This might have been a ruse to get all of us out of the house." They had left the doors and windows open.

"We'll soon find out," said Nancy.

Hurrying inside, she dashed to the telephone

and called the fire department. They had not been notified but said they would come at once.

Quickly Nancy and Bess locked all the doors and windows, and took the kitchen door key with them. As they ran through the grove toward the packing house, the girls noticed that blazes had sprung up here and there among the trees.

"This fire has been deliberately set!" Nancy declared. "Someone started it while the workers were at lunch." Immediately she wondered where Antin had been. Could he possibly be the arsonist and if so why?

When they caught up to George and Hannah, Nancy told them that the firemen were coming. She rushed up to a burly picker and asked how she could help.

"You're a girl," he said. "What can you do?"

Nancy was angry. She turned away. There was nothing she could do to save the orange packing house which was now a mass of flames, but she might be able to do something to preserve the trees. She ran over to Tina, who was sobbing, and asked her.

The woman pointed toward the river. "There's a hose and a pump down there," she replied.

Nancy did not wait to hear more. She quickly told Bess and George, and the three rushed off toward the river. It seemed as if trees were burning everywhere. They found the pump and hose, quickly unwound it, and turned on the nozzle.

Within minutes they were able to put out the fire in the nearby trees.

"Let's try another section," George suggested, and began lugging the hose forward.

Just then they heard the fire engines arriving. The girls, however, kept on with their own work.

In a short while two of the firemen came into the grove dragging a large hose. Suddenly they realized that the trees were already being hosed, and were astounded to see the job being done by three girls.

"Good work!" said one.

With the two steady streams of water, the rest of the fires in the grove were soon extinguished.

"Who's in charge here?" one of the firemen asked Nancy.

"The foreman, Antin Resardo. I think he's at the packing house."

"Let's get out of here," Bess suggested. "This place smells horrible."

The scent of scorched oranges mixed with burning wood was bad enough, but added to this was rank-smelling steam. The girls' eyes were smarting and they were covered with soot.

"We'll take care of your hose," said one of the firemen. "You'd better go to the house and bathe your eyes."

"We will," Nancy replied.

On the way back they met Hannah, who reported that the packing house was a complete wreck.

"It's a shame," she said. "The fire chief is convinced this was the work of a firebug."

Nancy said she thought the arsonist might be the enemy of Mr. Billington who had used his name to deliver the explosive oranges. "Whoever the person is he knows he's being pursued. He hopes to intimidate Mr. Billington into dropping the hunt by ruining his orange business."

The others agreed. Hannah said a neighbor had offered to let Mr. Billington use his packing house until he could build a new one. "Only I'm afraid there aren't many good oranges left."

When they reached the house Nancy said she must telephone her father at once. "I'll tell him what has happened so he can pass the word along to Mr. Billington."

Fortunately he was in his office and she quickly told the story. Mr. Drew was astounded.

"I'll get in touch with Mr. and Mrs. Billington immediately about coming down. Please stay there. I'll call you back."

Within half an hour Mr. Drew phoned. He and the Billingtons were leaving River Heights at once in order to make a quick plane connection in New York.

"We'll get to Melbourne about ten tonight," he said. "Please meet us, Nancy."

"Bess and George and I will be there," she promised.

Nancy reported the conversation to Hannah and the girls, then said, "I'd like to go back to the packing house and look through the ruins if they're cool enough. Maybe we'll find a clue to the arsonist."

Bess and George were eager to join her.

"Setting those fires was a wicked thing to do," Bess declared.

When the girls arrived at the water-soaked ruin, they walked around it, their eyes alert for any clue. Suddenly, in a heap of half-burned papers, Nancy spotted something that could be a clue. She bent down and picked up a scrap of paper.

"Look at this!" she exclaimed excitedly.

CHAPTER XI

Off the Market

THE partially burned newspaper which Nancy showed to Bess and George was a copy of the edition which held the name *Drew* in the code message.

"It's ringed with red crayon!" Bess burst out. "What does that mean?"

George made a guess. "I think the person who set the fire is a member of some gang out to ruin Mr. Billington's reputation and business. He's worried because Mr. Drew and Nancy have been brought in to solve the mystery."

Nancy agreed. "We have very few clues," she said, "and everything seems to be so disconnected. What we must do is find a motive for the whole thing."

Bess suddenly caught her breath. The other girls looked at her and asked, "What's the matter?"

Bess's reply was upsetting. "Suppose that fire-bug takes it into his head to burn down the house we're staying in!"

There was silence for a few moments. Finally Nancy said, "Perhaps we'd better go back and talk this over with Hannah."

When they reached the house, Tina and Antin were with Mrs. Gruen. Hannah became alarmed at the thought of another fire.

"I wish we had a good watchdog here," she said.

Tina was fearful of the house being set on fire, but Antin shrugged off the idea.

"What reason would anyone have for doing such a thing?" he asked Nancy.

She replied, "What reason would anyone have for burning down the packing house and setting fires in the grove?"

As she spoke, Nancy watched the caretaker's face intently. He showed no change of expression.

Nancy thought, "He certainly is a strange person." Aloud she asked, "What do you think is going to happen to Mr. Billington's orange business?"

Antin set his jaw. "That's up to Mr. Billington. I know what I'd do if it belonged to me—forget the whole thing. But of course I'll follow whatever orders he gives me." The foreman stalked from the house.

As it neared time for the girls to leave for the Melbourne airport to pick up Mr. Drew, Hannah confessed that she felt uneasy about staying alone. The Resardos had already left, saying they were going to Ruth's birthday party.

When George suggested that she come with the girls, Mrs. Gruen said, "I don't think I should go along and leave this house unprotected."

"You're absolutely right," said Bess. "Nancy, I'll stay here with Hannah."

Nancy and George set off. On the way George remarked, "Wouldn't you think after what happened here today Antin and Tina would have stayed home and waited for the Billingtons? They didn't even offer to pick them up at the airport!"

Back at the Billington house, Hannah and Bess were startled by loud knocking on the front door. Hannah went to answer it.

"Don't let anybody in!" Bess called out.

Hannah asked, "Who's calling?"

"Mr. Scarlett."

Mrs. Gruen opened the door and the man stepped inside.

"Where's Nancy Drew?" he asked abruptly.

"She's not here."

"Where did she go?"

Bess started to tell him, but Hannah gave the girl a warning look and answered for her.

"Nancy has gone on an errand. Do you have a message for her?"

Mr. Scarlett said indeed he did—a very important one. "Mr. Webster has taken his house off the market. It's no longer for sale. I must have the key to the house at once. Get it for me."

Hannah said she had no idea where it was. He would have to wait until Nancy returned.

"I can't wait," the realtor snapped. "I must have the key now." He turned to Bess. "She probably told you where it is. Bring it to me!"

"I don't know," the girl replied firmly. "When Nancy returns, I'll tell her you want the key. She can bring it to you in the morning."

Mr. Scarlett seemed nonplussed as well as angry. Before he had a chance to make any further demands, Hannah said to him, "That's all. Good night, Mr. Scarlett."

She held the door for him and reluctantly he went out.

Immediately Bess said, "Nancy's going to be dreadfully disappointed about the Webster house being taken off the market. I wonder what the reason was. I gathered from Mrs. Nickerson that Mr. Webster was eager to sell the place."

As they continued to discuss the strange turn of events, Nancy and George were bowling along the road toward Melbourne. When they were about halfway there, George remarked that a car was racing up behind them.

"That driver certainly is in a hurry," Nancy remarked, glancing into the rear-view mirror.

Instead of whizzing by, the car suddenly drove up alongside and the driver yelled, "Stop!"

Nancy suddenly recognized the driver and stopped her car.

"Mr. Scarlett!" she exclaimed. "What do you want?"

"The key to the Webster house," he replied. "Hand it over."

Nancy said she did not have it with her. She changed the subject abruptly and asked Mr. Scarlett who lived in the moss-covered mansion next to the Webster home.

"I don't know," he replied. "I've never been in there."

Nancy and George looked at each other but said nothing. Why had Scarlett lied?

The realtor came back to the subject of the key. "Give it to me!"

"I told you I don't have it with me," Nancy replied. "But tell me why you want the key. My father is coming down tonight and I need it to show him the house tomorrow morning. I'm sure he'll buy the place."

"It's no longer for sale," Mr. Scarlett snapped. "Mr. Webster has taken it off the market."

"What!" George exclaimed. "I understood he wanted to sell it as soon as possible."

"Not any more. Tell me where the key is and I'll go back to the house and get it from your friends."

Nancy had no intention of doing this. It had occurred to her that this whole story might be false. She would ask her father to get in touch with Mr. Webster direct and learn the truth.

"Hurry up!" Mr. Scarlett shouted.

Before Nancy had a chance to answer, a trooper on a motorcycle whizzed up and stopped. He pulled out a pad and pencil and said to Mr. Scarlett, "You were going way beyond the speed limit."

"I was in a hurry," the realtor replied.

George nudged Nancy and whispered, "Now's your chance to get away."

Nancy thought so too. Putting the car into gear, she drove off down the road.

George glanced back several times to see if Mr. Scarlett was following them. There was no sign of his car.

As they neared the airport, George said, "It seems strange he knew where to find us. Do you suppose he was at the house and Hannah or Bess told him?"

"Even if he were there, I'm sure they wouldn't tell him. Besides, they could truthfully say they didn't know where the key is because I hid it and forgot to tell you all the place."

Nancy parked and glanced at her watch. Ten minutes to ten.

"Dad should be in soon," Nancy said, a smile crossing her face. "It will be so good to see him again."

As the girls walked into the terminal building,

they noticed that people waiting to meet relatives or friends looked tense and worried. One woman was pacing the floor nervously, wiping perspiration from her face, though the night was cool.

As she came close to the girls, she said, "The New York plane is in trouble."

"What's wrong?" Nancy asked her.

The woman looked at the girl, terror in her eyes. "The landing gear jammed. The wheels won't come down. This means a crash landing!"

CHAPTER XII

Frustrated Thief

THE girls gasped and rushed outside to watch the plane carrying Mr. Drew and the Billingtons. It was circling the field. The runway had been sprayed with foam. A fire truck and an ambulance stood nearby. Soon the great jetliner began to descend.

"But the landing wheels aren't down!" murmured the woman who had followed the girls outdoors.

With Nancy and George she watched breathlessly. Upon landing the plane might spin around.

Fortunately the pilot made a skillful belly landing and all the waiting friends and relatives gave sighs of relief. Mr. Drew and the Billingtons were among the first to get off. The pilot had already come out and the two men hurried to catch up to him.

"Congratulations on your fine work!" Mr. Drew called. Mr. Billington also complimented the pilot.

"It's all in a day's work," the young captain answered with a smile, then disappeared into the offices of the airline.

Mr. Drew introduced the Billingtons, who said they had been looking forward to meeting Nancy and her friends. As soon as they were seated in the car, Mr. Billington requested that the girls tell him about the fire.

Nancy reported on it in detail and told him the arsonist had not been caught. "Mr. Billington, we have found Tina and Antin a complete mystery. Do you think it possible that he had anything to do with the fire?"

"Not Antin," Mr. Billington said quickly. "I always thought he loved my orange grove and would be heartbroken if something happened to it."

Nancy and George made no comment. Antin had certainly not shown this kind of regret about the burned trees and packing house.

George told about the girls' experience on the way to the airport. "Mr. Scarlett was positively contemptible, and he said that the Webster house had been taken off the market."

"Dad," said Nancy, "could you find out if it is really true?"

When he nodded, she added, "The girls and I

have wondered if Scarlett is acting in collusion with the owner of the moss-covered mansion." She told the men about the wild animals they had seen. "The trainer was very hostile to us. I suspect he doesn't want any new neighbors."

Mr. Drew asked, "Have you talked to the police about the place?"

"No, I haven't," Nancy replied, "but I'll do so first thing in the morning."

When the Drews and their friends arrived at the Billington house, they were amazed to hear of Mr. Scarlett's rude behavior toward Hannah and Bess.

Mr. Drew scowled. "I don't like his actions. I doubt that he is to be trusted. You say he went into the grounds of the moss-covered mansion furtively?"

"Yes," Nancy replied. "Suppose I call the police right now and ask if they can tell us anything about who lives there."

She phoned at once but was told she would have to wait until morning when the office with the local records was open.

The next day Nancy lost no time in getting the information. The old house had been purchased by a man named Fortin. He had been a trainer of wild animals for a circus. Fortin had received a permit to have the beasts there as long as they were properly caged. Nancy thanked the clerk and hung up.

"I wonder if Fortin was that tall heavy-set man with the whip," she said to Bess and George.

Nancy was more convinced than ever that Fortin was in back of the move to keep the Drews from buying the Webster house. He might have found out she was an amateur detective and did not want her so close. She might report that he allowed the dangerous animals out of their cages.

"I wish I could get inside that mansion," Nancy said. "I have a strong hunch there's something going on between Scarlett and Fortin which has a direct bearing on the Webster property."

Bess spoke up. "You'd better forget it, Nancy. We came down here to solve the mystery of the explosive oranges. Why don't we forget that place with the wild animals and go hunting for Hamlin orange groves as George suggested?"

"I'm ready to start," Nancy said.

The girls set off in the Billingtons' car. Nancy drove up one road and down another. Many people had small groves, others large ones, but none had Hamlin oranges. Most were apparently Valencias.

At last the girls spotted a big grove of smooth-skinned Hamlins. Nancy turned into the long driveway and went to the packing house. She introduced herself and her friends to the foreman, saying they were from the North and were interested in solving the case of the explosive oranges.

"My father is the attorney for Mr. Billington," she said. "I'm eager to find out which grove those particular oranges came from. Can you help me?"

The foreman, who told them his name was Tom Seever, smiled. He looked up at the darkening sky and said, "We'd better run into the packing house. I'll tell you what I know. Looks like a heavy shower coming any second."

The girls hurried after him and went into the shelter. Pickers from the grove and a visitor who had just driven in began rushing inside too. By the time the rain came down hard, the place was so crowded that moving around was impossible.

Suddenly the lights went out. A few seconds later Nancy felt a rough hand against her arm. She realized that someone was trying to cut the strap of her handbag.

Quickly she clutched the bag in one hand and with the other grabbed the man's wrist. Finding it, she pinched the flesh so hard that the purse snatcher cried out in pain. Instantly she could feel him moving away.

A few seconds later the lights went on. Nancy craned her neck to look at all the people who had taken shelter in the packing house. It was hopeless to try identifying the suspect, but she saw the visitor dash to a car and drive off. Was he guilty and had he followed her here?

The rain had stopped and the men had begun to file outside. Nancy and her friends were the last to leave the building. After talking to Mr. Seever for a few minutes about the mystery, she was convinced that there was nothing he could tell them which would cast any light on the case. All his oranges were sold to trustworthy buyers he knew well, and no fruit had been stolen.

The young sleuth asked if he would give them directions to another Hamlin grove.

He told her of one about a mile away and the three girls headed for Owen's Grove.

It was a large grove and there were many pickers at work. Nancy was directed to the office of the owner, Mr. Owen. It was in a small building that stood a short distance from the packing house.

She went to the door and asked, "May I come in?"

The owner rose, smiling, and said, "Yes, indeed. Won't you sit down?"

Bess and George had stayed outside to look over the packing house.

The young detective introduced herself. "My father is working on Mr. Billington's case. Since the explosive oranges that were brought into the Base were Hamlins, I wondered if you might possibly have a clue to help solve the mystery."

Mr. Owen said he did. "The FBI were here, of course, and I told them a suspicion of mine. One of my workers never showed up here after the affair. He was a strange, uncommunicative person by the name of Max Ivanson. We tried to get in touch with him where he boarded but were told that he had disappeared."

"Did he take anything from here with him?" Nancy asked.

Mr. Owen nodded. "Several sacks of oranges were missing. We think he took them. I've forgotten the number now but it corresponded to the count which the NASA authorities had listed in their report about the delivery."

Nancy was intrigued by this information. "What did Max Ivanson look like?"

Mr. Owen opened a desk drawer and pulled out a photograph. "This is the man. I just came across it."

Nancy tried not to show her surprise. Ivanson looked enough like Mr. Billington to be a brother!

"Can you tell me anything more about him?" Nancy queried.

"A little. Ivanson's a bachelor. He was a good picker but would never stay to work overtime."

Nancy arose. "You have been most kind and helpful," she said, putting out her hand.

Mr. Owen shook it warmly and wished her luck in solving the mystery. "I'm glad if I've been of help," he said.

Bess and George were excited when Nancy told them what she had found out, and discussed the clue as they started for home. A shortcut led them past the Nickersons' house.

"Let's go in," Nancy suggested, and turned into their driveway.

Both of Ned's parents were home and were amazed at all Nancy had accomplished, particularly her last clue. Then the conversation turned toward the Webster house and the moss-covered mansion.

"I certainly wish I could get inside that weird-looking place with the wild animals," said Nancy.

Mr. Nickerson grinned. All three girls thought how much Ned looked like his father when he smiled broadly.

"I think I just might arrange such a visit," Mr. Nickerson said. "I know a man who is an animal control officer in the Public Health Service. Perhaps he could make a routine inspection of the moss-covered mansion and"—he winked at Nancy —"perhaps he could take a secretary with him!"

CHAPTER XIII

Eerie Inspection

"WHAT an exciting suggestion!" Nancy exclaimed. "Think of going inside the moss-covered mansion!'

All the others agreed it was a good idea except Bess, who looked worried.

"Nancy, please think this over. You know the trouble we almost got into with those wild animals on the outside of the house. No telling what may happen if you go indoors."

Nancy turned to Mr. Nickerson. "Surely it can't be dangerous if the Health Department goes there regularly to inspect the place."

Ned's father nodded. "I can soon solve this," he said. "My friend Mr. Wilcox, the animal control officer, will know whether or not it's possible and also safe for you to go into the moss-covered mansion."

He went to make the call. While waiting, George said she was envious of Nancy's visit to the place. Bess remarked timidly, "Well I'm not. I don't mind telling you those animals frightened me half to death."

Mr. Nickerson soon returned, a wide smile on his face. "Everything is arranged. Mr. Wilcox will be here tomorrow morning at ten to pick you up."

"That's wonderful!" the young detective exclaimed. "I think we'd better dash home now. I'll see you at ten o'clock tomorrow morning. By the way, Mr. Nickerson, will you request Mr. Wilcox not to introduce me at the moss-covered mansion?"

"That's a good idea," he agreed. "If they know your name, you might not get a friendly greeting! Anyway, since you are not a regular member of the Public Health Service staff, let the people at the mansion think of you as Wilcox's Girl Friday."

This reference to the Robinson Crusoe story struck Bess funny and she began to laugh. "You'll be Mrs. Robinson Crusoe," she remarked. On the way home, however, Bess sobered again. "I just hope nothing happens to you!"

"I promise to keep my eyes open," Nancy told her friend.

She could hardly wait for the following morning to come, but during the remainder of the afternoon, Bess kept referring to the possible dangers Nancy might encounter.

Once she said, "Suppose that leopard mauls you!"

George looked at her cousin severely. "Will you

be quiet? Nancy is determined to go and I don't blame her. There's no point in trying to scare her away."

Bess said no more but Hannah Gruen did. She was inclined to agree with Bess. "I know Mr. Wilcox will be with you, but what protection would he be against an angry lion?"

When Mr. Drew and Mr. Billington heard what the plan was, they took a different attitude. Both were sure Nancy could not be harmed if Wilcox was with her.

The lawyer added, "I know you will keep alert, Nancy, and look in all directions at once."

Nancy bent to kiss her father and patted him on the cheek. "Are you trying to make me into some kind of a wonder of science?" she teased. "I've never learned to swivel my head!"

He chuckled, then said that he and Mr. Billington were going out to have dinner with Mr. Datsun.

"See you in the morning," he told the others and the two men set off.

The three girls went up to Nancy's room to help her pick the outfit she would wear the following morning. The choice was a white dress and shoes. Nancy would arrange her hair in a bun so she would look older.

Bess announced she was suffering with hunger pains so the trio went downstairs to have dinner with Mrs. Billington and Hannah. Once more the

Resardos were not there. The rest of the evening was spent reading the latest reports of the forthcoming flight to the moon.

"I see that there are going to be many celebrities here," Mrs. Gruen remarked. "Even the president may come down!"

The newspaper carried pictures of well-known press correspondents who had arrived to report the shoot. There were photographers by the hundreds and a sprinkling of visitors from other countries.

"It's going to be fabulous!" Bess exclaimed. "Aren't those astronauts who are on the mission handsome?"

"Yes, and remarkably brave and intelligent," George added.

Finally it was time for the group to retire. Nancy was too excited to drop off to sleep but eventually she did and woke up refreshed and ready for the day's adventure. After breakfast the girls drove to the Nickerson home. A few minutes later Mr. Wilcox arrived and was introduced to them. He wore a khaki smock-type suit.

"So this is the young lady who will accompany me," he said, smiling at Nancy, "and act as secretary for the trip." He handed her a stenographer's pad and a pencil. "Take lots of notes," he added with a wink.

Nancy laughed. "I understand. Some for you and some for me."

The two went to the car. Nancy noticed a pair of asbestos gloves on the seat.

"I wear those whenever I have to go inside a cage," he explained.

When they arrived at the moss-covered mansion, Wilcox turned into the narrow path that wound through the orange grove and the jungle to the house. He parked and they walked up the steps of the old-fashioned house.

The Public Health officer rang the bell. He and Nancy stood waiting but there was no answer.

"Maybe the bell doesn't work," Nancy suggested.

Her companion pounded loudly on the door. After a long while it was opened a crack. Nancy's heart began to beat a little faster. Would the huge man with the whip open the door?

Wilcox called into the crack, "Mr. Fortin?"

"Yes," came the answer. "No visitors allowed!"

"I'm Wilcox from Animal Control of the Public Health Service," he told him. "I have an order to inspect your place again. Here are my credentials."

All this time two dogs had been yelping and barking in the background. Mr. Fortin certainly had protection, Nancy thought.

"Wait until I tie up these animals," the owner said.

He closed the door and was gone so long that Nancy thought perhaps he was not going to let them in. Finally the door opened.

"No visitors allowed!" Fortin said sharply

Fortin was a slender man about fifty years old with a reddish complexion. It flashed across Nancy's mind that he did not give the appearance of an animal trainer. His hands were rather soft-looking, not like those of a person used to heavy work. He escorted the callers through the center hall and out to the kitchen. He opened a rear door which gave a view of the many cages backed up against the house just beyond the kitchen door. Nancy got her notebook ready.

"These cages look very clean and the animals well-kept," Wilcox remarked, and Nancy wrote this down.

She followed him outdoors and around the three sides of the cages which seemed to be well-constructed. Each had a sheltered area.

"Very good," said Wilcox.

All this time Nancy's eyes had been roaming around the jungle. She could not detect anything suspicious.

Fortin led the way back inside the house and headed for the front door. At once Wilcox spoke up. "I have orders to look over the whole mansion."

The owner frowned and said, "Why is this necessary? A license issued to me to keep the animals certainly doesn't permit the Public Health Service to pry into my private life!"

Wilcox replied, "Those are my orders. There

could be vermin in the house from those wild animals." Before Fortin could object, Wilcox started up the stairway. Nancy followed, then Fortin.

After a quick inspection of the second-floor rooms, Wilcox said, "Everything seems to be all right." He turned to Fortin. "I thought maybe you had some small animals up here."

"Well I don't!" Fortin snapped.

He started down the stairway, but Nancy held the health officer back. She whispered, "See that door over there? It probably leads to the third floor."

Her companion nodded. "I want to take a look upstairs, Mr. Fortin," he called and walked over to the door.

As Wilcox opened it, the owner's face turned red with anger, but all he said was, "You'll find nothing up there. It's an old tower."

Nevertheless, Wilcox climbed the stairs, with Nancy at his heels and Fortin behind her. The tower had windows which looked out on the ocean. In front of one stood a powerful telescope.

"That came with the house," Fortin explained. "It's so old I guess it was put in soon after the people built the place. They probably watched the ships at sea."

Nancy had walked over and looked through the telescope. She could plainly see the Space Center and the rocket that would take the astronauts to the moon.

"Everything okay?" Fortin asked in a sarcastic tone.

"Everything's okay," the Public Health officer replied, and Nancy wrote this down, along with her observations relating to the telescope.

As the visitors were coming down from the second floor, Nancy noticed a man in the lower hall. He was the big fellow with the whip! Instinctively she held the notebook partly across her face so that she would not be recognized.

When they reached the foot of the stairs Fortin ignored her. He introduced his associate to Wilcox as Joss Longman, saying he was the best animal trainer in the world.

Wilcox nodded, then checked through the first floor with Nancy. They found nothing suspicious. Back in the hall the two men were waiting for them sullenly.

"That's all now," Fortin said sharply and walked toward the front door, but Wilcox did not move.

"We haven't seen your basement yet," he said.

Hearing this, Longman turned quickly and hurried toward the kitchen. Nancy saw him open a door at the back of the hall and disappear.

Once more Fortin began to argue that the Public Health Service had no right to intrude on his privacy.

"Orders are orders," Wilcox said firmly. "Take me to your basement."

Fortin glared at the visitors, then he slowly walked to the kitchen. When they came to the door at the rear of the hall through which Nancy had seen Longman disappear, she put out her hand toward the knob.

"Don't go in there!" Fortin shouted at her. "That's a clothes closet."

Nancy doubted this but she followed him into the kitchen. Fortin began to talk about how old-fashioned the room was.

"That's only a coal stove," he remarked. "It's pretty hard learning to cook on it. As soon as I get more money, I intend to replace it with a modern range."

Nancy suspected that the man was stalling for time. He went on talking about the outmoded plumbing and what trouble they had with it. She was convinced that Longman had gone ahead to conceal something in the basement.

"What is it," she wondered, "that they don't want us to see?"

Finally Fortin opened a door in the kitchen and clicked on a light in the basement. He led the way down a steep flight of wooden steps. Longman was not in sight. Nancy was sure he had used a secret entrance to the place.

Wilcox had already started walking around the basement which contained nothing but old furniture and piles of rubbish thrown against the walls. This seemed odd to Nancy. The Public

Health officer did not act as if he suspected any-thing.

Fortin asked, "Well, are you satisfied now with your inspection?"

Wilcox looked stern. "I don't think much of your housekeeping," he replied. "Please see that the trash is cleaned out of here."

"Okay," Fortin growled.

The two men started up the stairway. Nancy, pretending that she was writing down what Wilcox had said, purposely leaned against a pile of old furniture. Presently the load shifted. Nancy grabbed a child's desk for support.

The next moment the whole conglomeration of furniture came tumbling down on her!

CHAPTER XIV

Outsmarting a Liar

THE racket caused by the falling furniture sent Wilcox and Fortin running back to the basement.

The animal trainer, instead of asking if Nancy had been hurt, said to her angrily, "What were you trying to do? You have no right touching anything around here! You were snooping, that's what. Talk!"

Wilcox said icily, "I'm sure she meant no harm. Are you hurt?"

By this time Nancy had picked herself up and though her clothes were dusty from the furniture, she had not been injured.

"I'm sorry, Mr. Fortin," she said. "I used to have a desk very much like this one. When I touched it, the whole pile came tumbling down."

Fortin's face was grim. Nancy thought he was going to say he did not believe a word of her story. Quickly she asked, "Is this desk for sale?"

"No!" the animal trainer almost shouted at her.

"And I'd appreciate your leaving. I have work to do."

Mr. Wilcox spoke up. "We'll go at once and I'll give the Health Service an excellent report about your animal operation here."

While Nancy brushed dust from her clothes, she took in every detail of the wall behind the pile of furniture. She had spotted a steel door. Evidently Longman had rushed downstairs to try hiding it with the pile of furniture. Something secret must be inside!

Nancy had also noticed heavy cables in the basement. One of them ran through the wall next to the half-hidden door.

Fortin said sarcastically, "Listen, miss, you're delaying my work. Please go at once."

"Oh I'm sorry," Nancy apologized and scooted up the stairway.

She was puzzled by what she had seen. The young detective had a strong hunch that something besides the training of wild animals for a circus was going on at the moss-covered mansion.

Mr. Wilcox and his "secretary" left the house and rode off. Nancy told him what she had seen in the cellar. "Why do you think Fortin was trying to conceal that door?"

Wilcox smiled. "I'm no detective, but I suspect he had something hidden behind it. Since I insisted upon seeing everything, he was probably afraid I might want to look in there. I'm sure no wild animal was inside. Otherwise it would have picked up our scent and made some kind of noise."

Nancy said no more and in a short time she and the health inspector reached the Billington house. She thanked him for his help and jumped out of the car.

Bess and George met her at the front door. "Thank goodness you're here in one piece," said Bess.

George asked, "Did you learn anything exciting?"

Nancy related her experience to the girls, Mrs. Billington, and Hannah Gruen. All of them tried guessing what might be beyond the steel door where the furniture had been piled up.

"Even though Mr. Wilcox doesn't think so," Bess put in, "I'll bet there's some kind of an animal behind that door."

"You could be right," Mrs. Billington said, frowning.

George had a different theory. "I'm sure Fortin only keeps those wild animals to scare people away and isn't training those beasts to perform. There's some other reason he and Longman are living at the moss-covered mansion."

"Like what?" Bess asked.

"There could be all kinds of secret rooms," her cousin replied.

Nancy was intrigued by this idea. "They might even be storing explosives!"

Bess stared at her friend. "Are you hinting that Mr. Fortin might have been responsible for the explosive oranges that were shipped into the Space Center?"

George answered. "I wouldn't put it past him."

Mrs. Billington looked worried. "If you're right and anything should go wrong, the whole of Merritt Island could be blown up!"

Nancy turned to Hannah. "You haven't said a word. What do you think?"

Looking worried, the housekeeper replied that their suspicions about the moss-covered mansion should be reported to the FBI.

Nancy pointed out, "But it's mostly speculation —we haven't any constructive evidence."

She also reminded the others that the FBI had a good lead about the person responsible for stealing the oranges and delivering them to the Space Center. He was Max Ivanson. The man had disappeared and not been found yet.

When Mr. Drew and Mr. Billington came in, the results of Nancy's visit to the moss-covered mansion were reported to them. The men were as interested in the story as the others had been. They had no solutions to offer.

Mr. Drew said that he had obtained a postponement of Mr. Billington's trial. "I have some other news, too," he added. "I found out there's no Tripp Brothers Circus listed. Of course that doesn't mean there isn't one. It may be too small and unimportant to be in the police information files."

"I'm sure," Nancy said, "that the whole thing is a cover-up for something sinister."

Bess sighed and changed the subject. "While you were out, Nancy, we had a call from Mrs. Nickerson. Ned and Dave and Burt will be down tomorrow."

Nancy's face broke into a smile. How glad she would be to see Ned! "And it will be great to have him help on the mystery," she thought.

Bess told Nancy that she and George had been busy laundering the girls' clothes, including Nancy's. "So we're all ready for the Nickersons' house party," she told her.

"You were sweet to do that," said Nancy. "Thanks."

She learned that Tina and Antin had the day off, so all the work had fallen on the others.

"Would you mind doing the marketing?" Mrs. Billington asked Nancy. "We need a number of things. Perhaps you three girls could go and divide the shopping list."

"I'd like to," Nancy replied. "By the way, do you have the Websters' new address?"

"No, I'm sorry I don't."

Nancy decided to stop at the post office on the chance she could get it. She said, "Mrs. Billington, I don't trust Mr. Scarlett and I'd like to check his story with the owner."

The girls drove to town and each went in a different direction to buy meat, vegetables, fruits, paper napkins and various other items.

As soon as Nancy finished her shopping, she walked to the post office. There she asked if she might have Mr. Webster's other address, and told why she wanted it.

The postal clerk smiled but said he was not allowed to give out such information. "If you wish to write a letter and mail it, I'll be glad to forward it."

"I'll think about that," Nancy replied and turned away.

A woman who stood nearby had heard the girl's request. Now she came up to her and said, "I'm a friend of Mr. and Mrs. Webster. I know their city address. Would you mind telling me in more detail why you want it?"

Nancy explained the complication about the couple's Merritt Island home and that she wanted to speak directly to Mr. Webster about its being taken off the market.

The woman smiled. She took an address book from her handbag and flipped the pages to W. Then she wrote down the address of her friends, the Websters, and handed it to Nancy.

"Thank you very much," Nancy said. "As soon as I get home, I'll phone them."

As the young detective was about to leave the

post office, she saw something that made her step back quickly. Walking along the street and carry-ing on an animated conversation were Mr. Scar-lett and Mr. Fortin!

"They *are* friends," she decided. "I wish I could hear what they're talking about."

This was not feasible because Scarlett would identify her and tell Fortin. Perhaps Fortin had already described her to Scarlett and he in turn had told who she was!

Nancy waited until the men were out of sight, then went to the Billingtons' car where the girls had arranged to meet. When Bess and George heard about the men, they agreed with Nancy that no doubt she had been identified.

"This means more trouble!" Bess prophesied.

As soon as Nancy reached home she telephoned Mr. Webster long-distance. He answered immed-iately. Nancy introduced herself and told why she was calling.

"I'm certainly glad you got in touch with me," Mr. Webster said. "I can't understand Mr. Scar-lett's actions. He has had no instructions from me to take my Merritt Island house off the market. I'll call him at once and set him straight."

"You may have a hard time finding him," Nancy remarked. "He says he's on vacation, and no one answers the doorbell at his house. However, I've seen him several times. Mr. Scarlett even chased me in his car while I was on my way to the airport to meet my father. He demanded that I return the key which he had lent me."

"You have the key?" Mr. Webster asked. "In that case, you keep it and go into the house as often as you please."

Nancy told him about her experiences at the moss-covered mansion. "Didn't the wild animals bother you?" she asked.

"No. In fact, I doubt they were there then."

Nancy mentioned the friendship between Fortin and Scarlett. Mr. Webster was amazed.

"It certainly sounds as if something phony is going on. I'll give your father a long option on the house and notify Mr. Scarlett he no longer has it on his list."

"That's very generous of you," said Nancy. "My father will be in touch with you."

Mr. Drew and Mr. Billington had gone out again. They did not return until dinnertime that evening.

"I have nothing new to report, Nancy," her father said. "How about you?"

Nancy told him of her telephone talk with Mr. Webster. The lawyer was delighted to hear of the long option on the Webster house. "I know that if the mystery of the moss-covered mansion can be cleared up, you'd like me to buy the place."

His daughter laughed. "I guess I'd like it anyhow, but I admit we'd certainly have strange neighbors."

"Who could be very dangerous," Bess put in.

Suddenly Hannah Gruen said, "Oh, I forgot!"

All eyes turned in her direction. She went on, "There was a personal in today's paper that caught my eye. Using the code words 1, 5, 9, and 13 the message read, 'Beam ready for action.'"

Each one at the table pondered the words. "What do they mean?" George asked. "This message is the hardest one yet."

The others agreed but no one had an interpretation to offer. After dinner Nancy sat down in a big chair in the living room and stared straight ahead of her.

Mr. Drew said, "That brain of yours is cooking up something. How about telling us what it is?"

Nancy told them she had come up with a daring idea to help solve the mystery. "Using the numbered words code, I'll run a personal in Sunday's paper. It will arrange a meeting for the people who are communicating through the personal column."

"That's a clever idea!" her father said. "I wish you luck."

Nancy found a notebook and pencil. She drafted message after message but was not satisfied with any of the combinations of words. The whole sentence must make sense as well as the code words.

Finally the others said good night and went up-stairs. An hour later Nancy heard the Resardos' car pull into the driveway.

"Oh dear! I don't want them to see these papers," she thought and quickly gathered them up.

When she reached her room, the young detective sat down to continue her work. Just as sleep was overtaking Nancy, a new idea for the wording of the personal came to her.

"I have it!" she told herself.

CHAPTER XV

Stolen Car

NEXT morning nothing was said about the personal which Nancy wanted to put into the newspaper. The Resardos hung around, so the others kept their conversation to inconsequential matters.

Finally Antin went off to the grove, presumably to see what fruit might still be saleable. Tina was unusually talkative. She assisted with all the work and even offered to help make the beds.

"Thank you but that won't be necessary," Hannah Gruen told her.

She was as eager as the girls to hear what Nancy had worked out on the code message. She kept Mrs. Resardo on the first floor, however, so the rest could go upstairs and talk out of earshot.

They gathered in Nancy's bedroom. Bess, bursting with curiosity, asked, "Nancy, did you finish the coded message?"

"Yes," she replied, and took a sheet of paper from her handbag. The others crowded around to see it.

"Does that sound innocent enough?" she asked her father.

"Very good, my dear," he replied. "I see you have underlined the vital words." He read it aloud:

" *'Meet round ship museum Monday twelve.'* "

"Where is that?" Mr. Drew asked.

Nancy explained it was in Cocoa Beach. "The museum has a replica of one of the Spanish Plate Fleet vessels which went down in 1715 off the coast of Cape Kennedy, then known as Cape Canaveral.

"One of the worst hurricanes on record drove the ships onto the rocks. Nearly everyone on board was drowned. Only one ship escaped and returned to Spain to tell the story."

Mr. Drew nodded. "At that time the Spaniards had conquered the Aztecs in Mexico and were robbing them of all their exquisite gold objects. These in turn were made into Spanish coins and packed in boxes and shipped to Spain."

Mr. Billington added, "Some of this treasure has been salvaged. The museum contains many gold coins and pieces of eight as well as other treasures. You'll be intrigued when you see them."

"Sounds great!" George said. "Nancy, I take it that you hope the coded message will be seen by the men involved in the explosive oranges mystery, and they'll gather outside the museum."

Nancy nodded. "Once we see who they are, we can report them to the authorities."

"That's right," Mr. Drew said. "Don't try capturing them yourself!"

Nancy laughed and said she would like to put the ad in the paper at once. "May I borrow your car?" she asked Mr. Billington.

"Yes indeed."

Mr. Drew smiled. "I have a surprise for you girls. Yesterday I rented a car for you to use during the rest of your stay here. It had to be serviced, so I said you'd pick it up this morning." He took the receipt from his pocket and handed it to Nancy.

"Wonderful, Dad!" she exclaimed, and kissed him. "Thank you loads. George and Bess can bring your car back, Mr. Billington."

"No hurry, Nancy. Your father and I have some work to do here on the case. We'll be around until after lunch."

The three girls left the house and drove directly to the newspaper office. Nancy handed in her coded message for the personal column and paid for it. She was assured it would appear the following day.

As Nancy and the other girls strolled outside, Bess asked, "What's next?"

Nancy said she wanted to tell Mr. Scarlett that

she had Mr. Webster's permission to keep the key, in case the realtor had not already been informed.

"We're not far from his office. Let's see if he's there."

She drove to it but found the door locked. She went to his home. No one answered the doorbell.

A woman in a neighboring yard called out, "The Scarletts aren't here. They drove off early this morning."

"Thank you," Nancy said. "I'll leave a note for Mr. Scarlett."

She took a sheet of paper from her bag and wrote down the message. Then she slipped it through the slot in the front door.

"When do we get our car?" George queried.

"Right now."

Nancy headed for the center of Cocoa Beach and drove to the rental agency. Bess and George waited for her while she went into the office. Nancy showed the receipt and the clerk led her to a parking lot at the back of the building. He pointed out an attractive tan station wagon.

"It looks new," Nancy said, delighted.

"It's practically new," the man told her. "I don't know why the owner wanted to sell it. Normally we don't buy private cars but this was such a good bargain we couldn't pass it up."

Nancy eagerly got behind the wheel and waved to the girls. George started the Billington car and headed for home. Nancy chose a different route.

She was making good time along the highway when suddenly a motorcycle roared up behind her. Riding it was a policeman.

"Pull over!" he ordered. "Let me see your license."

Nancy was sure she had done nothing wrong but did not question the officer. She showed him her license.

"Where did you get this car?" he asked.

Nancy gave the name of the rental agency and showed the receipt. The officer looked at her sharply, then said, "Are you aware you're driving a stolen car?"

The young detective gasped. "I certainly wasn't."

"Follow me!" the motorcycle policeman said. "We'll go back to that agency and see what it's all about."

The man in charge was shocked when he learned about the theft. He assured the policeman he was innocent, and explained that his company had purchased the car from an individual.

"What was his name?" Nancy asked.

"Rimmer," the clerk said. "Robert Rimmer."

The policeman said, "I suggest that you give this young lady another car and a new receipt."

The exchange was made and Nancy went on her way. When she reached home and told about the incident, Hannah Gruen began to laugh. "Nancy

Drew," she said, "it seems as if you can't go anywhere without having an adventure."

"But I just love it," Nancy replied with a broad grin. "Dad, have you any news?"

"No, I've been checking to find out if there has been any word on Max Ivanson. It certainly looks as if he's the one who carried the explosive oranges into the Base."

Mr. Billington spoke up. "And there's no clue to who set fire to the packing house and started the blazes in the grove. Ivanson might have done that too."

He added, "I'm well-covered by insurance, but a lot of time will be lost in building up a grove. You can construct a packing house fairly quickly, but you can't make an orange tree grow overnight!"

All this time Tina had been buzzing around, setting the table and going up and down the hall. Nancy suspected that the woman was not missing a word of the conversation.

Presently the Drews and their friends sat down to luncheon. Mrs. Billington asked, "Nancy, what time are the boys arriving?"

"We're to meet them at the airport at four o'clock," she replied. "By the way, we're not officially starting the house party until tomorrow. We girls thought it would be nice to give Ned a chance to visit with his parents before we all move in there. And Mrs. Nickerson agreed."

Soon afterward the girls began their long drive to the Melbourne airport. The plane was on time. Ned was the first of the boys to alight. Seeing Nancy, he rushed up to her.

"How's my little sleuth?" he asked, kissing her.

"I'm fine and have a million things to tell you."

Bess and George had found Dave and Burt. On the way to the Nickersons' the boys plied the girls with questions.

"We're going to start you working on the mystery Monday," Nancy told them. "At noontime we're to station ourselves at the Real Eight Treasure Museum and see if we can spot a few criminals."

"You mean it?" Dave asked.

Nancy explained her plan and the boys were eager to help.

Ned remarked, "Thinking up that coded message was pretty clever, Nancy."

"I only hope it works," she answered.

The boys were dropped off at the Nickerson home. They said they would come over to see the girls after dinner. "Is there some place we could all go and have fun?" Burt asked.

"I have an idea," said Nancy. "The Billingtons have a neat motorboat. Why don't we make use of it?"

"Good idea," Dave remarked. "I'll bring my guitar."

The three boys arrived at eight o'clock. Nearly

an hour was spent talking with Mr. Drew and the Billingtons. Since the Resardos were out, the mystery could be discussed freely.

"It sounds complicated to me," Dave remarked. "I'd like to have some time free from mystery. May we borrow your boat?" Mr. Billington nodded.

"I'll get the *Starbeam's* key," Nancy said. She had noticed it on top of the TV set.

The young people excused themselves and walked down to the dock. Nancy turned on the boathouse lights, then she and her friends climbed into the motorboat.

"Which way?" asked Ned, who had taken the wheel.

Nancy suggested that he turn right and cruise around a while, then come back and go past the Webster property.

Half an hour later they pulled up to the Webster dock. "The house!" Bess exclaimed. "It's all lighted up!"

Everyone was puzzled. Had Mr. Drew stopped in? Or was an intruder there?

"We'd better investigate," Nancy said quickly. "Ned, let's tie up at the dock."

He pulled alongside and the group scrambled out. While the boys secured the boat, the girls ran ahead. They had not gone far into the small orange grove when the lights in the house were extinguished one by one. When the visitors reached the back door, the place was in total darkness.

"Watch to see who comes out," Nancy called to Bess and George. She herself ran around to the front entrance. No one emerged from the house. By this time the boys had caught up.

"Do you suppose someone's hiding in there?" Bess asked Dave.

"Could be," he replied.

Nancy turned to Ned, who had found her. "Will you go back and use the phone in the boat? See if Dad is there and whether he has been here."

Ned hurried off. The others continued to watch the house, but nobody appeared.

Finally Ned returned. "Your father hasn't been here, Nancy," he reported. "But Mr. Drew said he'll be right over."

In a short time the lawyer arrived with Mr. Billington. "Did you bring the Websters' house key, Dad?" Nancy asked.

"No. None of us knew where you had hidden it," he answered.

"In my raincoat pocket," she said. "It's in my closet."

Mr. Drew had brought several flashlights which he distributed among the three couples.

"Let's look through the windows," Nancy suggested, and beamed hers through a front window.

"Oh!" she exclaimed. "The place is flooded with water!"

CHAPTER XVI

Misfit Shoes

"A PIPE must have burst!" Nancy cried out. "Oh dear! I wish I'd brought the key. We must do something fast!"

Mr. Drew decided to break a windowpane and crawl inside the house. Ned offered to do it and Nancy's father nodded.

"But go around to the back where the break won't show," Mr. Drew suggested.

Ned dashed off with the rest of the group following. As if about to punt a football, Ned made a run of several feet, lifted his right foot, and aimed it at a kitchen window.

Crash!

Ned reached inside, opened the latch, and raised the window frame. He pulled himself through the opening and unlocked the rear door. The others trooped inside. Nancy, making sure she was standing in a dry spot, clicked on the kitchen light.

Less than two feet away water was slowly flow-
ing toward her! The faucets in the sink had been
turned on full and water was pouring out. It was
spilling over the edge and cascading onto the
floor. George jumped forward and turned off the
faucets.

At once a search for the intruder began. Mr.
Drew called out, "Don't touch any switches if you
are standing in water!"

"I won't," Bess assured him. "I don't want to be
electrocuted."

Water had already flowed into the other first-
floor rooms. It was also spilling down the stairway. Burt and Dave rushed up to shut off faucets
in the bathrooms.

"Ned, let's look for the main valve and turn off
the water," Nancy suggested. "I think it may be in
the utility room."

The two dashed into the room adjoining the
kitchen. They found that the faucets in a sink and
a laundry tub had also been opened. Ned closed
them, while Nancy looked for the main valve. She
located it and turned off the flow.

When everyone assembled in the living room to
compare notes, each declared he had seen no sign
of the intruder.

"I guess he escaped by the front door before you
got there, Nancy," Burt stated.

Bess gave a great sigh. "I'd say we have an all-
night mopping job ahead of us!"

Dave grinned at her. "You forget I'm mop-up man for the Emerson football team. It won't take long. Let's go!"

Every broom, mop, and rag in the house was put to use. George and Burt found a couple of electric fans and plugged them in.

"Operation Dry-out is in good hands," Mr. Drew said with a grin.

He and Mr. Billington returned home ahead of the young people. The front light was on. As the two men walked up to the door, Mr. Drew bent down and picked up a shiny object.

"What is it?" Mr. Billington asked.

"A key. Someone must have dropped it."

Mr. Billington took the key. "This isn't ours," he said. "Why, look, it has the letter W cut into it."

"W?" Mr. Drew repeated. "Do you suppose it could stand for Webster? Maybe this is the key Nancy hid. Someone may have stolen it, then had no opportunity to replace the key, so he left it here."

When the men entered the house, Mr. Drew told Hannah Gruen about the find.

"That's strange," she said. "Nobody has come here this evening except the Resardos and they've been in their room all the time."

"Nancy hid the Webster key in her raincoat pocket," Mr. Drew remarked.

"I'll get it," Hannah offered.

Mrs. Gruen was gone only a couple of minutes, then returned holding the key. They compared it with the one Mr. Drew had found. It matched exactly.

"Queer things happen everyday," Hannah remarked. "I wonder what will be next."

Mr. Drew did not answer. He went to the telephone and spoke to the police captain about the flooded house and the key he had found on the doorstep. The officer promised to send a couple of men to the Webster house immediately.

Over at the soaking wet home the mopping-up operation was almost finished.

Nancy and Ned searched the house but found no clues to the intruder. While they were still hunting, the police car came in. Nancy spoke to the two men.

"The intruder must have had a key to this house," she said.

The police identified themselves as Needham and Welsh. They told of Mr. Drew's having found a key with a W on it near the Billingtons' front steps. Nancy and Ned looked at each other. Had Scarlett dropped it—or perhaps Antin?

As she and Ned walked to the rear of the house with the two officers, Nancy beamed her flashlight toward the river.

Suddenly she exclaimed, "I see some shoe prints!"

They stepped forward to examine them. "The

guy sure has big feet," Needham commented. "I think we should take plaster impressions of these." He requested his partner to drive back to head quarters for the equipment.

Nancy knelt on the ground and examined the prints, which went toward the water. Did she imagine it or were they wobbly looking as if the person was unsteady on his feet?

"Or," Nancy thought, "did the intruder deliberately put on shoes much bigger than his feet to disguise his size? He even took long strides and that too could account for the wobbliness."

She and Ned and Officer Needham followed the prints. Possibly the vandal had hidden a small boat among the bushes along the shore. The three made a thorough search but the only boat around was the Billingtons'.

The officer stopped to look at it. "She's a beauty!" he said. "It's a good thing that intruder didn't help himself to it!"

"It's locked," Ned said, "and I have the key in my pocket. Apparently the vandal escaped in his own boat."

By the time the searchers had returned to the house, Officer Welsh had come back with the plaster cast kit. While he was working, Nancy and Ned took his partner through the house, pointing out the damage.

The officer made a lot of notes and said the case would be put on the police blotter at once and a search started for a tall man with long feet. Nancy mentioned her own theory about his wearing over-size shoes and Needham was impressed.

"That's an idea," he said. "I'll jot it down."

Just then Officer Welsh came in. He said he had completed his work and if Needham was ready they might as well leave. House lights were turned off and the front door slammed shut.

As Nancy and her friends trudged through the orange grove and down to the river, Burt remarked, "We boys didn't have to wait long after our arrival for some excitement."

"It always happens," Bess added. "I vote that for the rest of the evening we forget about detective work."

She had hardly said this when George and Burt, who had started ahead, cried out in dismay.

"Our boat's gone!" George exclaimed.

The others ran to the dock. They could not believe their eyes. Mr. Billington's motorboat had been securely tied and Ned had locked the motor.

"There's only one way it could have been taken," Nancy spoke up. "It was towed away!"

"By whom?" Dave asked.

No one had an answer. A few seconds later Bess gave one of her great sighs. "It's a long trek from here to the Billingtons' house."

"It sure is," George agreed, "but let's get started."

Nancy said, "You all go and ask Mr. Billington

to call the police about the stolen boat. Ned and I will stay here a while. I want to hunt for clues to the thief."

The other four hurried off. With her flashlight Nancy searched for footprints.

"Here they are!" she cried gleefully. "The thief was the same person who was up at the house!"

Ned looked at her, puzzled. "But how could he have been? We were down here after he'd gone and our boat was still at the dock."

Nancy pointed out that the man could have towed the boat away when the police and everyone else were in the house.

"Or he might have been hiding up the shore a distance and a pal came to pick him up. Together they tied Mr. Billington's craft to a motorboat and went off."

Just then they heard a motorboat in midstream. "Let's hail it!" she said. "Maybe the pilot passed our boat."

Ned shouted lustily. The pilot heard him and slowed his motor. He steered for the Webster dock and called out, "Somebody need help?"

Quickly Ned explained. The pilot said he had not seen the stolen craft, but added, "How about hopping in here and we'll look for it?"

Nancy and Ned did not need a second invitation. As soon as the motorboat pulled up to the dock, they climbed in.

CHAPTER XVII

Tear Gas

NED introduced Nancy and himself. Their teen-age pilot said his name was Bud Musgrove. As his small motorboat sped along, they looked into every cove and indentation of the river, going up one side, then starting down the other. So far there had been no sign of the Billingtons' craft.

"I'm sorry," Bud said. "You say you have the key to the motor, Ned. Then the person who took your boat might have known about it and has a duplicate. Have you any idea who he is?"

Instantly Nancy thought of Antin, but said nothing. Was he accustomed to borrowing the craft whenever he pleased?

She asked herself, But why should he have gone to the Webster home? As Nancy was trying to puzzle this out, Ned suddenly exclaimed, "I think I see our boat! Over there at that rickety old dock."

Bud headed for the spot. A house on the property had burned down. The area was secluded.

"It's a good place for someone to hide a stolen boat," Nancy thought. "And for a thief to hide too!" Aloud she said, "Cut the motor! Quick!"

Bud obeyed. In the sudden silence Nancy spoke softly. "The thief may be hiding there, too. Let's go quietly and take him by surprise!"

The momentum of the craft carried it along quietly as Bud steered toward the dock. He pulled alongside the stolen boat.

"No one's in it," Ned announced. He looked around. "I guess this has been abandoned." He pulled the key from his pocket and jumped in.

Nancy was about to follow, but Bud held her back. "Better wait and see if the *Starbeam* starts."

Ned turned on the motor but there was not a sound. He tried again and again without result.

"That thief probably tampered with the boat and now it won't run," Nancy remarked. "Is the motor warm?"

"No," Ned replied, "so the *Starbeam* must have been towed here."

Bud jumped into the craft and together he and Ned examined the engine while Nancy beamed a searchlight on it.

Finally Bud said, "Several parts are missing. You won't be able to run this boat until they're replaced. I'll tell you what. Let's tie it to the back of my motorboat and I'll tow you home."

"Great! Thanks," Ned replied.

When they arrived at the Billingtons' dock Nancy invited Bud to come in.

The young man smiled. "Sorry, but I'm supposed to be on my way to a party. My date will think I've fazed her out."

The group at the house was amazed when they heard Nancy and Ned's story. Mr. Billington called the police to report that the boat had been found.

He said to the others, "I'm certainly burdening the authorities lately. We make at least one call a day to the police!"

Everyone smiled and Nancy thought, "We've come up with a few clues for them, too!"

Bess told Ned that his mother had phoned and was preparing a midnight snack for the young people. She was hoping the girls would move over there at once to start the house party officially.

"I'm all for that," Bess added, "Tonight's adventures have given me a tremendous appetite."

George teased her cousin. "You'd have had an appetite without any adventures."

The three girls hurried upstairs and packed the clothes they would need for the next few days. When they were ready to leave, Nancy promised her father she would keep in touch with him and the Billingtons to exchange news about the case. Mr. Drew said he would contact Mr. Webster and tell him of the vandalism.

"I'll ask him if he wants to have someone in town take care of it or if he'd like me to."

As he kissed his daughter good night, Mr. Drew wished her luck in getting results on Monday to her personal advertisement.

"Maybe you'll find out who the members of the gang are. Anyway, my dear, watch your step."

Nancy and Ned rode in the rented car, while the others took the Nickersons'. Despite the fact that the official opening of the house party lasted until almost two o'clock, none of the young people slept late the next morning.

After they had attended church services, Dave suggested that the whole group take a tour of the Space Center that afternoon. The others agreed.

Nancy was just as intrigued by her second visit to the Base as she had been before. The boys were especially fascinated by the rocket soon to lift off for the moon.

George, who had been silent for several minutes, said, "I'd like to be an astronaut. What do you think my chances are?"

"Oh no!" Bess exclaimed. "Suppose you went to the moon and got stranded there!"

Smiling, Nancy remarked that she too would like to become an astronaut.

Ned grinned and said, "How about letting us boys go first? We'll tell you how it is."

The bus driver, who had overheard the conversation, seemed to be amused. He turned slightly and said, "You boys had better get started on your training. While you're here, why not go for a physical checkup and briefing?"

"Great!" Burt replied with a wink.

George leaned forward in her seat. "What about me? Could I get the same treatment?"

"I think so," the driver answered, grinning broadly.

The others looked at Nancy. "How about you?" Ned asked.

"Perhaps," she replied, knowing they were kidding her. "After this case is over."

In a short time the bus reached the Vehicle Assembly Building. The tourists went inside. They were told about the immense structure and what took place there.

Then the guide said, "The space vehicle that will lift-off for the moon Tuesday was transported from here to its launch pad several weeks ago."

Nancy and her friends were the first to leave the building. They wanted to get a better view of the huge spaceship.

As they were coming out the door, two men, heavily bearded, came up to them. "Pardon me," said one. "We're doing an article on the moon flight for a science magazine. Would you mind if we take your picture, and quote what we over-heard you say on the bus about wanting to be astronauts?"

The six young people looked at one another but did not answer.

"Over here," said the second man who had a large camera. "We won't use your names."

He led the way around the corner to the side of the building away from the tourists.

"I guess there's no harm in it," Ned whispered to Nancy.

She nodded and followed the two men down the far side of the building. While one arranged the group against the wall with the girls in front, the other man focused his camera.

"All ready," he said.

His companion dashed out of the way and the photographer clicked his camera. Instantly a stream of tear gas shot toward them. Nancy and her friends tried to run, but their eyes began to smart and they could not see.

In the distance the guide was calling out, "All aboard!"

Nancy heard running footsteps and assumed their attackers had fled. As the fog of tear gas dis-sipated, Nancy was able to see dimly, but not well enough to move very fast for fear of bumping into something. She realized, however, that a man was coming toward her.

He proved to be one of the guards from the

A stream of tear gas shot toward them

Vehicle Assembly Building. Rushing up, he asked, "What happened?"

Nancy choked out the answer. "Tear gas! Two men with beards. One man had a camera that shot the stuff at us."

"Follow me!" the guard said. "We'll give you something to soothe your eyes."

"My friends too!" Nancy told him.

She could vaguely make out the rest of her group. Nancy called to them to follow her.

By the time they reached the front door of the Vehicle Assembly Building, the bus had gone. Nancy said there was a chance the attackers were on it.

"Hadn't you better phone the Visitors Center and have the bus checked?" she asked the guard.

"I'll do that at once—that is, as soon as I find someone to take care of your eyes."

Suddenly Nancy remembered the young engineer who was a relative of Hannah Gruen's. She asked, "Is Herb Baylor around? I know him."

"I'll get him," the man promised, and hurried off.

When Herb Baylor saw Nancy and the rest of the group and heard what had happened, he instantly took them to the infirmary where a young doctor gave them first aid. He put a few drops of a soothing solution in their eyes which soon relieved the burning sensation.

There was a knock on the door and the same

guard walked in. He was holding two wigs with beards attached and a box camera. "I found these at the side of the building," he said.

Nancy gasped. "The men who used the tear gas must have been wearing them!"

Ned added, "Now we can't describe those villains and they'll get away easily!"

"Too bad," Herb remarked. "What was their motive?"

George answered, "To scare us into dropping our detective work. But they can't do it!"

CHAPTER XVIII

A Ruse Works

HERB Baylor thought Nancy and her friends should return to the Nickersons at once. "Take it easy," he advised.

The young people were glad to and went to bed early. By morning everyone felt fine. A few hours later they set off for the Real Eight Museum of Sunken Treasure, reaching Cocoa Beach by five to twelve. Quickly Ned parked out of sight of the front entrance. Nancy and her friends took up positions behind posts on the covered patio of the octagonal-shaped building.

Exactly at twelve o'clock a car pulled in near the entrance. A few moments later a second one drew up behind it. Then a third and a fourth automobile stopped. A man got out of each car and the four assembled on the broad walk leading to the building.

Nancy's heart was pounding. One of the men was Scarlett, another was Antin!

"So Antin *is* one of the gang," she thought.

There was a heavy-set stranger. "That must be Max Ivanson!" Nancy decided. "He looks very much like that photograph I saw."

The last person to come toward the building was a young man.

Nancy thought, "Could he be the 'son' in the personals? His face looks familiar. Why do I think I know him?" Then it suddenly dawned on her. He strongly resembled Mr. Fortin, the owner of the moss-covered mansion.

The men came closer and then stopped to talk. Nancy could hear them plainly. Each inquired about who had written the personal in Sunday's paper. When all of them denied having done it, looks of fright spread over the men's faces.

"I'll bet the FBI found out about our code," said the heavy-set man. "I'm leaving!"

He ran to his car and the others fled to theirs. Moments later they roared off.

"Shall I chase any of them?" Ned asked.

Nancy replied, "Try Ivanson."

Ned and Burt rushed off and soon were out of sight.

Meanwhile Nancy had raced inside the museum to telephone her father. She paid the admission fee and dashed into a booth. Mr. Drew was astounded at what Nancy had discovered.

"I'll inform the police of this development," he told her. "They will certainly question Antin and search his room. I'll also clue the authorities in on who the other men are that may be responsible for the explosive oranges."

Nancy had remembered to jot down the license numbers of the men's cars and now gave these to her father. "Good work!" he said.

When Nancy emerged from the phone booth, Dave and the other girls stood waiting and demanded to know what was going on. In whispers she told them.

"Oh, Nancy," said Bess, "you've all but solved the case!"

Nancy did not think so. George was eager to go to the Billington house to learn the climax.

"But we have no car," Nancy replied. "We don't know when the boys will be back. Meanwhile, since we've all paid our admission, let's look at the exhibits."

A young woman came up to them and said, "You forgot to take your tapes and earphones. The tapes tell you all about the exhibits. Start on the left."

They went back to a counter where she handed each of them one of the little boxes to hold. They plugged in the tiny earphones. The tour began.

In the center of the room stood a replica of one of the ships dashed to pieces on the Florida coast in 1715. The old-time vessel had sailed entirely under canvas and for this reason was no match for a violent tropical storm.

Around the circular wall was a panorama of the history of cargo carried aboard these Spanish vessels that sailed between the homeland and the New World. The treasures on display were from ten of the eleven vessels in the ill-fated Plate Fleet.

As Nancy listened to the tape she learned that the Spaniards had subdued the Aztec Indians and made slaves of many of them. They were forced to work their gold and silver mines and fashion the metal into Spanish coins, jewelry, and other objects. Overseers were often cruel and the slaves worked long hours.

Other scenes showed gold ingots being packed into boxes, and gold and silver coins in others. Moving on, Nancy and her friends listened carefully to the running account on their tape recorders. Many of the objects on exhibit, such as sabers and sword handles, dishes and bracelets, were encrusted with coral.

Nancy found Bess rooted to one of the glass cases. "Isn't that pathetic?" she asked, pointing to a small wedding ring imbedded in coral. "It's so little a tiny woman must have worn it. Maybe she was the wife of one of the captains."

George walked up. She had heard Bess's remark and said, "I can't find much sympathy for those people. They were just plain thieves."

Nancy commented, "They certainly ruined the

Aztec civilization, which in many respects was far above that of their conquerors."

Before leaving the museum, Nancy and her friends went into the gift shop. The articles for sale fascinated them. Everyone bought pieces of jewelry made from gold or silver dug from the bottom of the ocean.

Nancy purchased a lovely necklace of pieces-of-eight coins for her Aunt Eloise in New York. She decided on a bracelet made of silver coins for Mrs. Billington, and a large piece-of-eight pin for Hannah Gruen.

After the young people had looked at everything in the shop, they left the building. Ned and Burt were just returning.

"Any luck?" George asked.

"No," Ned answered. "All the men disappeared in the next town. We couldn't find them or their cars."

"Let's go home," Nancy urged.

Bess insisted that they eat lunch before going to the Billingtons'. The boys found a lunch stand. Everybody was ravenously hungry except Nancy. She tried to hide the fact that her curiosity was getting the better of her but her friends sensed it.

"I'll eat this hamburger as fast as I can," Bess told her.

Nancy laughed. "Don't get indigestion!"

She ordered a lobster-salad sandwich and declared it was the best she had ever eaten.

"No dessert!" Ned spoke up. "I know Nancy's itching to leave and I am too!"

When they pulled into the driveway of the Billington home, a police car was there. Nancy and her friends hurried into the house.

There was wild confusion in the living room. Tina was screaming at a policeman that her husband was innocent of any wrongdoing. Antin was shouting that he was the victim of a frame-up.

At that moment a policeman and an FBI agent came down the stairs. The FBI man was carrying a bomb which he said had not yet been activated. The officer held supplies used in constructing homemade bombs. Nancy and her friends were told that Tina and Antin were attempting to move their possessions out when the officers arrived.

After advising the couple of their constitutional rights, the agent asked, "Mr. and Mrs. Resardo, if you're innocent, how do you account for these things?"

Instead of replying, the couple tried to make a dash for the front door. They were quickly stopped and brought back, but refused to admit anything.

Nancy whispered to the detective, "May I ask the prisoners a question?"

"Yes, go ahead. But of course they don't have to answer without having their own lawyer present."

The young detective looked directly at the Resardos. "Who set the fire in Mr. Billington's grove?" There was no response.

She tried another approach. "Is Max Ivanson a pal of yours?"

This question startled the Resardos, but they remained silent. Seconds later the prisoners were taken to jail.

Hannah Gruen gave a great sigh. "I'm glad they're gone," she said. "Imagine their making bombs right in this house!"

"Please don't talk about it!" Bess begged. "It makes chills go up and down my spine."

She wandered outdoors, more upset than she wished to admit. Dave had followed her and suggested that they all do something pleasant and get away from the mystery for a while.

"Like what?" she asked.

Dave thought for a moment, then said, "How about going to the Webster house to see if it has dried out yet?"

Bess liked this idea and so did the others. They climbed into the rented car and Ned slid into the driver's seat.

When they reached the Webster place, Burt said, "We couldn't see much of the grounds in the dark last night. Let's walk around now."

The boys were intrigued by the unusual trees in the garden, particularly the sausage tree. Everyone went over to it.

Suddenly they heard snarling in the jungle on

the other side of the fence. The young people shrank back just as the leopard came running from the direction of the cages.

"He's loose again!" Bess cried out.

Directly behind the animal was Longman with his whip. He kept snapping it against the ground and shouting to the beast. The leopard paid no attention. Snarling and hissing, the agile beast climbed the fence.

The next moment he made a flying leap across it and landed in the sausage tree next to the young people.

CHAPTER XIX

The Mansion's Secret

Branches of the sausage tree broke from the leopard's weight. They crashed to the ground, together with several of the hard, twelve-inch melons.

Screaming, Bess dashed toward the Webster house. She kept urging the others to follow her.

"Run! Run!"

Longman, on the other side of the high fence, seemed stunned for a couple of seconds. Then he cried out, "Catch this and slash that beast!" He tossed the whip to the boys.

Nancy, to avoid being recognized by the animal trainer, turned and ran to the house. In the meantime Burt and Dave had each grabbed a broken branch with the heavy sausage-shaped fruit and were ready to ward off the animal if he should attack.

As Ned caught the whip, he yelled to Nancy and

George, "Open the garage door! We'll chase the leopard in there!"

This was easier said than done. At first the leopard refused to come down from the tree. Then, responding to Longman's commands, he made a great leap toward the fence, but missed it and dropped to the ground.

Ned cracked the whip in the air and on the ground. The beast started to make another leap, then stopped. Lowering his head, he looked balefully at Burt and Dave and crouched as if about to spring at them. The two boys waved their tree-branch clubs in the air. By now the leopard was thoroughly confused.

With Ned working the whip and his friends flourishing their fruit-laden branches, the frightened beast was finally driven into the garage. Quickly George and Nancy yanked down the door.

Inside, the leopard set up a fearful racket. Above the loud snarls, the young people heard Longman call, "Keep him there! I'll get my van!"

While they were waiting for the trainer to come, an idea suddenly came to Nancy. She said to Ned, "This is our chance to get into the basement of the moss-covered mansion and find out what's behind the steel door. Will you go with me?"

Ned's eyes opened wide in amazement. "You mean ride in the van with the leopard?"

"Of course not," Nancy answered. "After the

animal is inside and Longman is in the driver's seat, you and I can quickly climb up to the roof of the van and lie flat. He won't know we're there and we can get off before he opens the van door."

Ned replied, "You know you're taking a terrible chance, Nancy. But I'm game to go with you."

To the surprise of everyone, Bess came speeding up the driveway in their car. They had assumed she was in the house.

She jumped out and said excitedly, "I brought some meat with a tranquilizer in it."

"You what?" George asked.

Bess explained that she had noticed a doctor's sign on a house in the next block. She had driven over there and explained to him what had happened. He could not come himself but had given her the chunk of raw meat with a tranquilizer pill imbedded in it.

The others stared at her in amazement. Finally Nancy said, "That's wonderful, Bess. It was quick thinking."

Dave took the chunk of meat. As the others carefully lifted the garage door a couple of inches, he poked the food inside. Then the door was shut tight again.

The enraged animal apparently sniffed at the meat, then ate it, because for a few minutes there was silence. Again he began to howl objections, but this time they did not last long.

"Bess, you're the heroine of the occasion!"

George told her cousin. She grinned. "And you know I don't say that often."

The others laughed, heaving sighs of relief. When they saw Longman's van coming, Nancy and Ned moved to another side of the house, so she would not be seen by the animal trainer. Bess and George followed.

As he jumped down, Burt told him that they had tranquilized his leopard. He looked at the boy disbelievingly. "How?" he asked.

Burt explained what Bess had done. "That tranquilizer should keep your animal quiet for a while."

"Very good." Longman looked around and asked, "Where are your friends?"

No one answered his question. But Dave said quickly, "Let's get to work. You'd better move the leopard to your place before the tranquilizer wears off."

"That's right," said Longman, and opened the rear door of his van.

The young people saw that a cage had been fitted inside. Longman opened the gate to it.

Burt and Dave rolled up the garage door gradually, in case the leopard was not asleep as they thought. This precaution was unnecessary, for the beast lay peacefully on the floor. It took the combined strength of Longman and the two boys to lift the leopard into the van. Then the cage gate and the van door were locked. The animal trainer murmured something that sounded like "thanks," and swung himself up into the driver's seat.

Instantly Nancy and Ned came from hiding. In a jiffy they had climbed to the van's roof and lay face down. By holding onto each other with one hand and grabbing bars along the sides with the other, the couple felt reasonably secure. Silently their friends watched them leave, hoping for safety and success.

Fortunately there was no one on the road to observe the two stowaways. The van turned into the grounds of the moss-covered mansion. When it reached the fence at the house, Longman got down and unlocked a gate. Then he drove through. The gate swung shut and locked itself.

Nancy saw a clump of bushes which would make a good hiding place. She whispered to Ned, "Here's where we get off."

The van was going so slowly toward the animal cages that the couple accomplished this easily without being injured. Instantly they dodged behind some bushes.

After Longman had unloaded the leopard, he secured the beast's cage with a double lock. Then he drove off.

"Now what?" Ned asked Nancy.

"I'm sure there's an outside entrance to the basement," she said. "Let's see if we can get in."

Luck was with them. They found a narrow door on the opposite side of the house. It was unlocked!

"Someone may be in there!" Ned cautioned in a whisper. "Let me go first."

Carefully he pushed the door open. It made no sound. The couple stepped inside. They were in the large basement room where Nancy had come with Inspector Wilcox.

The first thing she noticed was that all the debris had been moved away from the walls. Several doors were revealed. On tiptoe she and Ned walked toward the first one and Ned opened it. The place was well lighted and before them was a swimming pool filled with steaming, boiling water!

Nancy and Ned looked questioningly at each other. What was the pool used for? they wondered. Ned quickly closed the door. They moved to the steel door where the load of furniture had fallen on Nancy two days earlier.

In the room beyond, also well lighted, was an amazing laboratory. A complicated-looking machine with a dish-shaped parabolic reflector stood in the center of the floor. It faced the outside wall, which was made of glass building blocks.

"What is it?" Nancy whispered.

Ned walked around the machine, squinting at the various parts. He came back to Nancy and said, "Unless I'm all wrong, it's a very powerful transmitting antenna—a beamer."

"You mean some kind of signal is sent out from down here?" Nancy asked.

"Yes," Ned replied. "The telescope you told me about that's in the tower may act as a sighting device. It could locate the exact bearing and elevation of an object to be destroyed by the beamer."

Nancy was horrified. The telescope was aimed directly at the rocket scheduled for lift-off the next morning. She also thought about Antin's phone message regarding R-day. Instead of meaning Ruth, it could have referred to Rocket day.

"Ned," she said quickly, "would you know how to deactivate this machine?"

"I can try," he said. "But Fortin would have time to fix it before the launch."

"Meanwhile we could send the police here," Nancy told him.

Ned found some tools on a workbench near a series of wall cabinets. He worked with the tools for several minutes.

Presently she and Ned heard voices. To their amazement they were coming through a loudspeaker in the ceiling.

While listening, Nancy felt that no doubt Fortin, if it was necessary, could barricade himself in the laboratory and listen to conversations taking place upstairs. It would be a means of finding out how trustworthy his fellow conspirators were.

The couple recognized two voices as those of the tear-gas assailants at the Space Center. Nancy and Ned learned that Fortin was a clever and well-known scientist who had once been connected with NASA. He had become imbued with the ideology of a foreign power and was now using an assumed name.

He had entered into a conspiracy to undermine the U. S. space program and had agreed to cause great damage at the Center and to wreck the moon rocket. To accomplish this he had a spy working with the men in top-secret procedures. From this traitor Fortin had obtained the secret signals for the exact frequency and modulation for lift-off. In this way he could set his beamer to destroy the rocket.

Nancy whispered tensely to Ned, "He'll be murdering the astronauts!"

Just then Fortin spoke up. "Scarlett," he said, "I'm paying you off but not so much as I promised if you had done a good job."

Scarlett whined, "I did the best I could. I discouraged people from looking at the Webster house, but when Nancy Drew arrived, she was determined to see it. I pretended to go on vacation but she found me. I flooded the place to keep the Drews away, but she discovered it in time to avert any great damage."

"That's enough," said Fortin. "Ivanson, you certainly bungled that explosive orange deal. You were supposed to put those oranges around in strategic spots, so the lift-off would be delayed until my beamer was perfected. Luckily I have it ready in time."

Ivanson said belligerently, "You don't know what it feels like passing yourself off as somebody else even if I look like him. Fortunately they didn't examine the oranges while I was there. I guess Billington delivers lots of oranges to the Base, and since I had his truck, they must have thought the delivery was all right. I had no chance to drive around, though. A guard got aboard and directed me to the Space Center food supply depot and made me leave the sacks there."

"Here's your money," said Fortin. "Get out of here and never let me see you again."

A younger voice spoke. "Dad, I want to leave and go far away. I'm through!"

Fortin laughed. "You couldn't take care of yourself, son. You haven't been able to hold a job. I kept you away from here and even forbade phone calls so you wouldn't be involved if anything went wrong. You did think up that great father-son code but that backfired. We don't know yet who figured it out. But you came here to hide in case it was the FBI."

Young Fortin was not to be put down so easily. "If you expect me to stay, you've got to get rid of every one of those wild animals. You know they scare me to death."

Longman shot back, "We need those wild animals here to protect us."

"What's the latest news on Antin?" Fortin asked.

His son replied that a newscast had reported both the Resardos were in jail.

"What!" the scientist shouted. "There's no telling what they'll say to the authorities!"

"I can assure you," said one of the tear-gas attackers, "they won't talk. I made it pretty plain that if they ever did, their lives wouldn't be worth a nickel. And don't forget, boss, the Resardos did some good work. They stole those photographs and passed them around to us so we'd recognize Mr. Drew and the girls and their boy friends.

"Antin found out where they were going so we could watch them. Stevie here and I fooled them completely at the Vehicle Assembly Building and knocked them out with tear gas."

During the ensuing conversation Nancy and Ned learned that it was Max Ivanson who had started the fires in the Billington grove.

"Another stupid idea," complained Fortin.

Ivanson defended his actions. "I thought Drew would get scared and send his daughter and her friends home, but nothing shakes that bunch loose."

Scarlett grumbled, "Until Nancy Drew came along, we had the charge of the explosive oranges pinned neatly on Billington."

Nancy whispered to Ned, "I think we'd better go before some of those men come down here. Besides, we should notify the authorities at once!"

The two tiptoed to the door through which they

had entered. They were taken aback when the huge form of Longman appeared in the opening.

"You!" he cried and reached up to push a button on the wall. An alarm sounded upstairs.

"Let us out!" Ned demanded.

The towering Longman looked at the couple in amusement. "We have a special treatment for snoopers."

Nancy and Ned tried to break past him, but his huge, powerful body blocked the doorway like a stone wall.

Within seconds footsteps pounded down the stairway from the kitchen. Fortin appeared, leading the rest of his gang.

He glared at Nancy. "So you finally found out my secret. But you won't have a chance to tell anyone else. Ivanson, you and Stevie take these young detectives,"—he sneered—"and put them in the room with the steaming pool!"

CHAPTER XX

Countdown

EXERTING every bit of resistance they could, Nancy and Ned tried to escape from their captors. But their efforts were futile. They were shoved toward the room with the boiling pool and put inside.

"That's what happens to snoopers!" Fortin shouted excitedly. "I won't be thwarted in what I intend to do!"

The heavy door was swung shut and locked. The captured couple was forced to hug the wall since the ledge around the water was only six inches wide.

"Oh, Ned, I'm so sorry," Nancy said. "It's all my fault. I never should have asked you to come to this place with me."

"I certainly wouldn't have let you come alone," he replied. "Let's not give up hope of rescue."

Nancy nodded. Surely as soon as their friends realized Nancy and Ned had been gone too long, they would make a search.

"Only I hope they won't be captured as we were!" she worried.

Nancy and Ned tried changing their positions but almost tumbled into the water. To keep their balance they stood as straight and immovable as wooden soldiers.

"Something's got to break soon!" Ned remarked. "Maybe some of our captors will be afraid of a worse charge if they're arrested and the authorities find us in this pool. One of them may open the door."

No one did, however. Nancy and Ned assumed the men had left the basement. As the couple shifted their gaze, they noticed two tiny barred openings in the walls near the ceiling. One evidently admitted fresh air from the outside, the other from the basement.

Meanwhile, back at the Webster house the other young people were becoming more and more alarmed about their missing friends. Burt and Dave paced up and down the front yard. Bess nervously rumpled her hair, then smoothed it out and in a few seconds repeated the operation.

Finally George burst out, "We've got to do something! I just know Nancy and Ned were caught in a trap!"

The rest agreed. "We've waited long enough," said Burt.

Bess offered to drop the others off at the moss-

covered mansion. "I'll drive over to the Nickersons and get help."

When they reached the entrance, George and
the two boys got out of the car and set off along
the winding road that led through the jungle.
They listened and watched carefully.

"Do we dare pound on the door?" George asked.

Both boys vetoed this idea. "We'd surely be
captured," Dave replied.

By this time Bess had reached the Nickersons.
When Ned's father heard her story, he immediately rushed to the telephone. First he called Mr.
Drew and Mr. Billington, who notified NASA
headquarters. He reported the group's suspicions
regarding the activities of the occupants in the
moss-covered mansion, and the disappearance of
Nancy and Ned.

"We'll send men at once," the man at NASA
promised.

Mr. Billington telephoned the local police, who
also said they would rush to the suspected house
immediately.

Twenty minutes later, just as Nancy and Ned
felt completely discouraged, they heard a loud
commotion outside.

"Open up!" came a shout.

The couple heard no reply, but moments later
there was a stampede of footsteps on the stairway
to the basement. Fortin's voice rang out, "Police!

NASA agents! FBI! Open the secret lock, Longman! Let the animals loose!"

The pounding on the front door became more insistent and a voice cried out, "Open in the name of the law!" Inside the house the two dogs were barking madly.

The noise, coupled with Fortin's orders to release the wild animals, made chills go up and down the spines of Nancy and Ned.

"This is horrible!" she wailed.

Her remark was followed by screams from outside the house. Then came a roar. Had the animals attacked the law-enforcement men?

Suddenly there was silence in the basement. Moments later a voice called out, "Nancy! Ned! Where are you?"

Mr. Drew!

"Oh, Dad," Nancy cried out, "open the door that's below the vent near the ceiling."

Within seconds the heavy door was unlocked and opened. Nancy and Ned had inched along the ledge of the steaming pool and now literally fell into the arms of their waiting friends.

Bess gave a scream of horror. "Oh, you might have fallen into the boiling water!"

Nancy and Ned were pretty shaken by their experience, but recovered in a few minutes.

"Who's with you?" Nancy asked.

"FBI and NASA men and the police," George replied.

Quickly the couple reported what they had overheard before being captured. "I think I've deactivated the machine in the laboratory, but a NASA expert had better check," Ned said.

He walked over to open the heavy steel door to the laboratory. It would not budge. They all looked for a way to unlock it but could not find any.

"Let's go upstairs," Mr. Billington suggested. "I want to see what's happening."

They hurried to the kitchen and watched from a window. There was a great deal of excitement on the grounds of the moss-covered mansion. Tranquilizer guns were being used on the escaping animals. Finally all of them quieted.

Longman came from the house with a policeman and one by one they dragged the beasts into their cages, then locked the gates. Looking around furtively, Longman tried to escape but was caught and taken indoors.

The Drews and their friends found that the suspects, handcuffed, had been herded into the living room. Nancy and Ned were asked to come forward and tell the officers what they knew.

Before beginning, Nancy looked over the assembled crowd. Fortin was missing!

"The ringleader—the scientist—isn't here!" she exclaimed.

Nancy was assured that the man could not have left the house because it had been surrounded.

"Then I believe he's hiding in his laboratory," she stated.

Nancy led the NASA and FBI men downstairs, while the police stayed to guard the other prisoners. Engineers from the Space Center tried to unlock the steel door but concluded it must be fastened inside.

Nancy and Ned pleaded with them to break in. "I tried to deactivate the beamer that's going to destroy the rocket," he said, "but I can't be sure I was successful."

One FBI man suggested that they use a steel drill, but a NASA engineer said, "No. Vibrations might set off the beamer."

Nancy caught her breath. Suppose Fortin had decided not to wait until the next day to use his nefarious machine! He might blow up the rocket at any minute!

Quickly she told about the telescope in the tower which she and Ned believed was part of Fortin's setup.

Ned added, "Perhaps it's a sighting device to locate the exact bearing and elevation so Fortin can aim the parabolic reflector antenna in his workshop."

"We'll go right up there," one engineer stated. He and the two FBI men hurried to the third floor.

Meanwhile, the other NASA man put a radiation detector against the steel door. The results were negative.

Nancy and Ned returned to the living room. The saboteurs waived their constitutional rights to have a lawyer present and confessed their guilt. All were taken to jail except Longman.

"He will remain here with two detectives until the authorities can make arrangements for the wild animals to be moved," said one of the policemen.

The trainer told them he had become involved in Fortin's sabotage plan after forging the scientist's name on some bank checks. To avoid arrest, he had acceded to Fortin's demands that he care for the animals and keep intruders away.

"Fortin is a brilliant man," Longman went on as the other prisoners were led off. "But Fortin became obsessed with some dangerous political ideas and joined a radical group. I'm glad he's going to be prevented from doing the terrible thing he planned."

George asked Longman about the boiling pool. "Did Fortin build it?"

"Yes. It was one of his cruel ideas to dispose of intruders in case his animals didn't get them."

The trainer was questioned about how the authorities could get into the laboratory but he declared he did not know. They also asked him if Fortin could destroy the rocket from his basement laboratory. Again Longman insisted he did not know.

Guards were left at the moss-covered mansion inside and out. Two FBI agents had been stationed in the basement. Periodically they tried to persuade Fortin to give himself up but there was no response from inside the laboratory.

The Drews and their friends had mixed feelings about the mystery. It had been solved, but the instigator of the dreadful plot might still be able to destroy the rocket and possibly the three astronauts as well.

When they reached the Nickerson home, the young people were bombarded with questions by Ned's mother. She took a sensible view of the whole matter.

"I'm sure that if there is the slightest bit of doubt about the safety of those astronauts, NASA will not allow them to climb into the rocket."

Harboring this comforting thought, everyone went to bed feeling a little better. They were up and dressed by six the next morning. During breakfast they watched the television news. According to the report the moon shoot was planned for nine o'clock and at the moment all systems were go.

When the young people reached the building where the news media offices were located, they signed in. Together they walked out to get into buses and were taken to the Press Site.

"What a huge place!" Bess remarked.

The structure was really a large covered stadium. On each tier were long counters containing telephones. Behind them were rows of chairs, each one numbered. Nancy's group climbed the steps and found seats which had been assigned to them.

Men were bustling about, many with cameras, some with tape recorders, others with portable typewriters. Nearly everyone had binoculars.

In front of the Press Box was a long open lawn beyond which the Banana River gleamed in the sunlight. Near the shore, television and newspaper cameras had been set up by photographers. Across the river on Merritt Island stood the rocket, about three miles away, with condensed moisture, caused by the liquid oxygen, pouring from the base of it.

Every few minutes there would be an announcement and the young people would hold their breath. Was the countdown still on and would the rocket take off?

"Oh I hope Fortin was captured and had no chance to use a secret device to hurt the astronauts!" said Bess.

"I hope so too," Nancy replied.

There was a long wait before lift-off time. Nancy asked Ned if he would go with her to inspect the various trailers she had noticed off to one side of the Press Box. They went down and were told that these contained the broadcasting stations. Stepping across numerous cables, the couple walked along the row, then turned back. Behind the Press Box they found a snack bar.

"Let's grab a bite," Ned suggested.

While he bought hamburgers and milk, Nancy tried to phone the Billington house, but all the circuits were busy. When she and Ned returned to their seats, they learned that their friends had also been down to get a second breakfast.

As the countdown drew nearer zero, everyone who had been wandering around came to take their seats. Typewriters were clicking everywhere and cameras with telephoto lenses were busy.

Nancy wondered if ever again she would be so excited. Some time later she encountered another mystery, *The Quest of the Missing Map*, which also brought her some harrowing adventures.

It was five minutes to nine. The countdown for the moon shoot proceeded. Finally the announcer called out the final seconds:

"Three . . . two . . . one . . . zero!"

There was a burst of orange, green, and yellow gases from the base of the rocket. As it zoomed upward, enveloped in a varicolored cloud, the noise was ear-splitting and the grandstand shook as if a giant hand were shaking it violently.

"It's off!" someone shouted.

Nancy and her friends were holding hands, their nails pressing into one another's palms.

"Nothing is wrong so far!" Nancy thought, as

a white vapor trail formed behind the spaceship. "Oh, I hope—I hope—"

The rocket curved slightly and in a few moments disappeared among the clouds. Bess said shakily, "Ev-everything's A-OK!"

Seconds before this, a shout of triumph had gone up from the onlookers. Nancy and her friends did not cry out. Instead they were silently saying prayers of thankfulness.

When Nancy was breathing normally again she picked up the telephone in front of her. The main switchboard connected her with the Billington house.

Mr. Drew answered. "I knew it was you," he said. "Everything's A-OK here too. Fortin finally gave himself up, and his spy was caught. The transmitting antenna was ruined. The news was immediately telephoned to the Cape. This is why the astronauts were allowed to climb into the rocket and it was able to lift-off on time."

"Oh, Dad, that's wonderful!"

The lawyer chuckled. "You'll be interested to know that Fortin blames his failure on your detective work. But I'm terribly proud of you!"

Eye a mystery . . .

Read **NANCY DREW** girl detective™

All-new stories in this *New York Times* bestselling series

Have you solved all of Nancy's latest cases?

Pit of Vipers

Getting Burned

Troubled Waters

Read them all!

The Orchid Thief

Close Encounters

Visit www.SimonSaysSleuth.com for a complete list of Nancy Drew titles, activities, a screensaver, and more!

Aladdin Paperbacks • Simon & Schuster Children's Publishing • A CBS Company
Nancy Drew © Simon & Schuster, Inc.

If you like reading Nancy Drew, you'll love playing Nancy Drew PC mystery adventure games!

As Nancy, you'll step back to quaint 1930's small town America to solve a sinister mystery involving theft, deception and double-crossing. Dare to play *Nancy Drew: Secret of the Old Clock!*

Hurry—before time runs out!

Go to **www.HerInteractive.com** or call 1-800-461-8787 to order. Available in stores now!

#1 PC Adventure Game Series in America!

Collect all the award-winning Nancy Drew mystery games

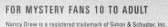

FOR MYSTERY FANS 10 TO ADULT

Nancy Drew is a registered trademark of Simon & Schuster, Inc.

Created by

Match Wits with The Hardy Boys®!

Collect the Complete
Hardy Boys Mystery Stories®
by Franklin W. Dixon

The Hardy Boys Back-to-Back
#1: The Tower Treasure/#2: The House on the Cliff

Celebrate over 70 Years with the World's Greatest Super Sleuths!

Match Wits with Super Sleuth Nancy Drew!

Collect the Complete
Nancy Drew Mystery Stories®
by Carolyn Keene

Celebrate over 70 years with the World's Best Detective